TRANSFORMERS ONE

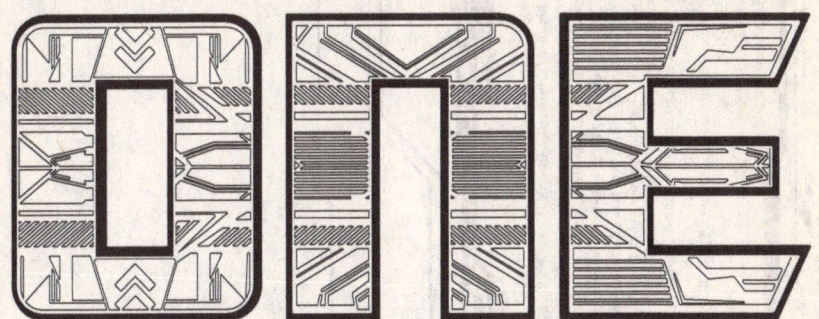

MOVIE NOVELIZATION

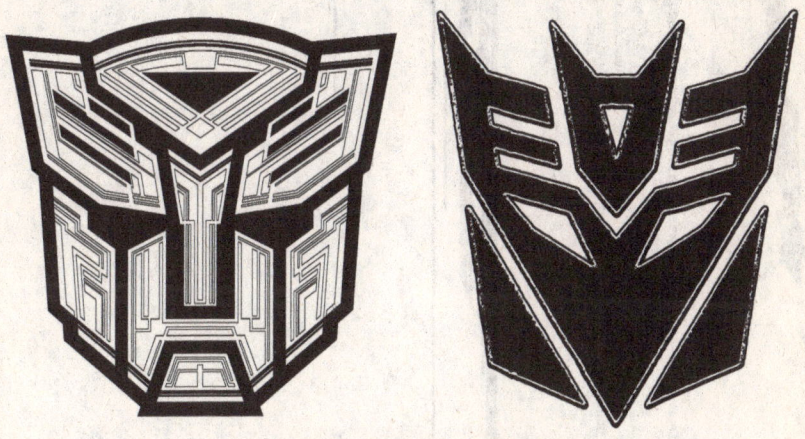

Adapted by Ryder Windham
Based on HASBRO'S TRANSFORMERS™ ACTION FIGURES
Story by ANDREW BARRER & GABRIEL FERRARI
Screenplay by ERIC PEARSON and
ANDREW BARRER & GABRIEL FERRARI

Simon Spotlight
New York   London   Toronto   Sydney   New Delhi

SIMON SPOTLIGHT
An imprint of Simon & Schuster Children's Publishing Division
1230 Avenue of the Americas, New York, New York 10020
This Simon Spotlight edition August 2024
TRANSFORMERS and HASBRO and all related trademarks and logos are trademarks of Hasbro, Inc. © 2024 Hasbro. © 2024 Paramount Pictures Corporation.
All rights reserved, including the right of reproduction in whole or in part in any form.
SIMON SPOTLIGHT and colophon are registered trademarks of Simon & Schuster, LLC.
Simon & Schuster: Celebrating 100 Years of Publishing in 2024
For information about special discounts for bulk purchases, please contact Simon & Schuster Special Sales at 1-866-506-1949 or business@simonandschuster.com.
Designed by Nicholas Sciacca
Manufactured in the United States of America 0724 OFF
10 9 8 7 6 5 4 3 2 1
ISBN 978-1-6659-5935-3 (pbk)
ISBN 978-1-6659-5936-0 (ebook)

Chapter 1

Here goes nothing, Orion Pax thought as he ducked past an empty security station on a high level within Iacon Tower. The tower was in a nice area of Iacon City, an enormous underground metropolis on the metal planet Cybertron. Orion tiptoed through a dark corridor, quietly opened a sliding door, and entered the city archives, a vast chamber with walls that were lined with large computers.

Orion moved deeper into the chamber. All the lights were off, but he knew his way around. The archives' computers and databanks held extensive information about Cybertron. Orion was curious by nature, and he had a special interest in Cybertronian history.

The only problem was that the archives were in a restricted area, and Orion wasn't supposed to be anywhere near them at Iacon Tower. Ever.

Like all Cybertronians, Orion was a bot, a living robot. His bulky, bipedal metal body was clad in blue and red armor plating, and his rectangular identification badge was displayed on the upper left side of his chest. Although he had been alive for many cycles, he was young for a Cybertronian.

Older Cybertronians were known as Transformers robots. They had conversion cogs in the center of their chests, and the cogs allowed them to transform their appearance. They could easily change from their *bot modes* to their *alt modes*, alternative forms such as cars, heavy-duty vehicles, or aircraft. Transformers robots also had many opportunities for work and could choose where they wanted to live in Iacon City. Some Transformers bots lived in luxury residential complexes and didn't work at all.

But young bots like Orion did not have conversion cogs and were unable to convert. And because cog-less bots could not change into vehicles with wheels, treads, or wings, they had limited options for getting around Iacon City. They could either walk on their own two legs or take public transportation, such as the high-speed trains and shuttles that traveled throughout Iacon City.

As for work, cog-less bots had no choice. All of them worked in the Energon mines.

It's not fair, Orion thought as he moved deeper into the archives.

He knew his work in the mines was important. Energon was the preferred fuel of all Cybertronians and was vital for keeping everyone alive and healthy, whether they had cogs or not. For many generations, Energon flowed freely on Cybertron, but fifty cycles ago—before Orion was born—Energon stopped flowing. The only way to obtain Energon was for miners to harvest it from deep inside the planet.

Orion frowned. *Why do all the cog-less bots have to be miners? Why can't I be something different, something . . . more?*

As much as Orion didn't like being a miner, he did appreciate that the top of his head was equipped with a standard mining lamp, because it helped him see in the dark nooks and crannies in the archives. He had often wandered the archives without anyone noticing, but today his cleverness would be put to the test.

Orion stopped in his tracks, hearing the loud footsteps of what could only be two large security Transformers robots.

I must've tripped the alarm, Orion thought. Quickly, he used his headlamp to search the room for a place to hide. He shifted its beam across the floor and found an open ceiling board. He jumped into the ceiling and turned his headlamp off.

"See anything?" one the guards asked the other.

"Nope. Told you this was a waste of time. No one comes up here," the second guard said, annoyed with his partner.

"Then why's the alarm tripped?" asked the first guard.

The second guard shrugged. "How should I know? Why does this library even have an alarm?" he asked.

"This is the archives," the first guard corrected.

"Who cares. No one is going to steal any of these worthless things. Let's go." The second guard led the way.

The first guard sighed as he followed his partner off of the archive floor. "I really wanted to get my hands dirty," he said.

"You'll get your chance," the second guard reassured him, "just stay positive."

The coast is clear, Orion thought. He swung a cable to the floor and climbed down, making sure he didn't make any more noise. After a few moments Orion felt safe enough to continue his search. He switched his headlamp back on and scanned the shelves. A handful of discs caught his eye. *One of these has to have something worthwhile.* Orion grunted, thinking about what the guards had said. Orion didn't believe that everything in the archives was worthless. But the heavy layers of dust made him wonder if any other bots ever used the archives.

"Okay, let's see what we've got here," he said to himself as he flipped through the discs in his hand. "Seen it, seen it, ooooh." He paused. "This is new." He inserted the disc into a nearby projector, switched off his lamp, and listened.

A bright hologram appeared above the projector and filled the room. The hologram was an image of a Transformers bot with an array of magenta prongs that extended above his angular head. Orion recognized the Transformers robot, and he gasped.

It's Alpha Trion, one of the thirteen Primes!

The hologram of Alpha Trion faded away and was replaced by a new hologram, an image of a point of light. Orion watched with amazement as the light grew brighter and expanded into an illuminated silhouette, a geometric figure with a head, two arms, and two legs. Orion was still studying the figure when Alpha Trion's recorded, disembodied voice announced, "At the dawn of time, there was our gracious and powerful god, Primus. To protect our universe, Primus chose to sacrifice his life force, transforming himself into our planet, Cybertron."

The illuminated figure of Primus crouched and changed into a bright ball of light. Alpha Trion continued, "From within Cybertron's core, Primus birthed the first Transformers, known as the Primes."

Orion saw the image flicker, and then the holograms of the thirteen Primes rose from the place that he knew as the Well of Sparks, the birthplace of all Cybertronians. From what he had learned on his previous visits to the archives, Orion could identify each of the thirteen Primes. Prima, Zeta, Micronus, Megatronus, Solus, Alpha Trion, Quintus, Amalgamus, Leige Maximo, Vector, Onyx, Alchemist, and Nexus.

Alpha Trion continued his speech. "The Primes were the most powerful Transformers, appointed to watch over and protect future generations. To assist them, Primus created an entity of great power . . . the Matrix of Leadership."

Just then, a hologram of the Matrix of Leadership appeared as a glowing sphere bracketed by curved handles. Orion watched the Matrix levitate out from the Well of Sparks and glide directly into Zeta Prime's chest. Orion couldn't help smiling. Zeta Prime was his favorite Prime.

"With the Matrix in the Primes' possession," Alpha Trion said, "Cybertron's natural power source, Energon, flowed in abundance, sustaining life across the planet. Until that one fateful day, when the Matrix was lost and Energon no longer flowed in abundance, sustaining life across the planet. For generations, there was peace and prosperity . . ."

Suddenly a veil of darkness fell over all the light in the hologram. It was three large ships. Orion recognized these from his other findings in the archives. These were Quintesson ships.

"Until the Quintessons descended from the skies. The Great War began." Alpha Trion's voice boomed on. "The Primes were decimated by three alien invaders, and the Matrix of Leadership was lost." The hologram became garbled and fragmented as the image of the Matrix fell and broke apart. The holograms crackled and flickered off.

"That's it?" Orion huffed, frustrated. "But

where's the Matrix of Leadership now?" Unfortunately, he had no time to ponder his disappointment. The lights on the floor turned on. Orion dove into a corner, hiding as the two guards searched the archives again.

"I swear I heard something. Someone's in here," the first guard said.

The second guard agreed this time. "I think you're right."

They searched each aisle and then came upon the area Orion was hiding in. Not so well, at that. Orion didn't completely fit in the corner he was in. His legs were all but revealed. The two large security guard Transformers bots lumbered toward him. When the guards came to a stop, they were close enough to Orion that he could see the conversion cogs in their chests. Orion was caught. "Who are you?" the first guard asked suspiciously.

"Oh, hello!" Orion said, trying to play it casual. "I'm so glad you're here. Which way is the exit? I must've taken a wrong turn. Is it that way, or . . ." Orion stood up then, making it clear to the two guards that he was not a Transformers robot.

"Check this out. He doesn't have a conversion cog," the first guard said mockingly, his finger pointed at Orion's chest. "A trespassing no-cog. Why aren't you down in the Energon mines, mining Energon, like a good little Energon miner."

Orion held a casual look on his face, but deep inside he resented those words. He kept it cool and said, "I should be, thank you. Pleasure meeting you both . . ."

The guards kept their eyes on Orion. "You're under arrest," the first guard said.

"Fellas, I was just watching historical records, for a good reason," Orion began. "These archives could hold clues as to where the Matrix of Leadership is . . . or . . . *or* explain why my entire generation was born without cogs," Orion reasoned.

"I'm going to strike him," the first guard said with a smile. He had been waiting all night.

"It's way more satisfying on the run. Let's give him a head start." His partner laughed.

"Good idea," said the first guard. "It's not like he can *transform*." Now the two guards both laughed.

"Oh yeah?" Orion challenged. "Watch *this*." Orion bent down and shifted his arms. Still wondering whether Orion could actually change his form, the guards stepped back, giving him space to move. That's when Orion sprang forward and ran off as fast as he could.

The guards realized that Orion had tricked them, and they were furious. They snarled as they began chasing after him through the archives.

Orion darted up the aisle and yanked the cable he had brought down from the ceiling; the ceiling grates fell and smashed the two guards on their heads. Orion continued to slide around a corner in search of a device he had come across before that could help with his escape.

"Where is it, where is it?" he wondered as he frantically searched the shelves. The two guards gained on him as he grabbed an old drone camera and tossed everything else on the shelf onto the floor between him and the guards.

Forced to continue their chase in the air, the two guards converted into their flying-jet alt modes. Orion pounded on the camera drone he'd snatched, trying to get it to turn on.

"C'mon, c'mon, work!" he yelled.

Just then, the drone sputtered on and started to take flight. Orion beamed with pride right before he dove through an open window. Although Iacon City was entirely underground, the city's gleaming towers illuminated the cavernous darkness and not only rose from the vast metal cavern's floor but dangled like stalactites from the expansive metal ceiling.

The towers' lights appeared to glide past Orion as he fell. The old camera drone wasn't enough to make him catch flight, but it was enough to soften his fall. He tumbled past a dangling structure's wall before he struck and bounced off a rooftop. He rolled across the roof, slid over the edge and down a steep lower roof, and toppled into a ceiling vent. He fell through the vent and crashed into an office filled with tall, stylish-looking Transformers robots. He saw that most of the office's interior was made from sparkling gold. Because he knew such places were off-limits to miners, he felt embarrassed to be there. He pushed himself up from the floor and tried to act casual as he gazed upon the high-class Transformers bots.

"Oooh, Energon..." He gawked. "Evening. Hi. Pardon me," he said politely as he moved past gleaming Transformers robots who looked down at him with disdain.

Orion rushed through the exit. He emerged onto a street that was crowded with more sophisticated Transformers. When a group of Transformers bots nearly kicked him as they walked by, Orion thought they just hadn't noticed him, but then he realized they might have been trying to kick him out of their path. In Orion's experience, Transformers bots were seldom kind to cog-less bots.

Orion ran onto a train platform. A long train was passing below, and Orion leaped toward one of the train's cars. He landed face down on the car's transparent roof. Through the roof, he could see the heads and shoulders of the tightly packed passengers. All were cog-less bots, and each carried a heavy drill.

Energon miners, Orion thought as he gripped the edges of the roof. *Just like me.* He recognized several miners who were part of his crew. A few miners looked up and saw him. Because Orion had a reputation for getting into and out of trouble while exploring Iacon City, the miners were amused but not surprised by his antics.

The train carried Orion and the other miners away from the bright central area of the city. Orion tilted his head and looked back. If the two guards were still flying after him, he couldn't see them.

Soon the train was speeding through a run-down area of Iacon City, where buildings were layered with rust and crud, and all the lights were dim. The train began to slow down as it approached a depot. It was still slowing when Orion released his grip on the roof, slid off the train's side, and jumped down to the platform.

Just then, a buzzing noise from above caused him to look up. He saw the two flying guards descending fast toward him. In mid-air, the guards flipped and changed fast into their bot modes. The moment their heavy feet landed on the train platform, they ran straight for Orion.

Orion was out of breath as the train came to a stop beside him. As the two guards approached, running full speed in their bi-pedal alt modes, one shouted, "Don't move!"

"Fellas, let's not overreact here," Orion joked. It looked like he was caught. But before the guards could grab Orion, a dolly full of mining equipment crashed into the two guards.

"Hey! Watch where you're going!" an angry mining bot with gray armor and yellow eyes shouted.

Now distracted, the two guards turned their attention to the miner. "What did you say, no-cog?" asked the first guard.

"Oh, sorry, I didn't . . ." The gray bot trailed off, faking concern.

The guards looked around and noticed Orion was missing. "Where'd he go? Where's that miner?" the second guard asked frantically.

The gray-armored miner stated the obvious for the two guards. "This is the miner sector, lots of miners here. Oh, there's one, there's another one. . . . ," he said.

"Don't get smart," the first guard snarled. "He's red and blue and running like a dirty criminal."

"Red and blue? Yeah, I saw him. He went that way." The gray miner pointed off in a random direction and sent the guards running toward it.

Right before the train departed the platform, the miner pushed his dolly onto the train and into a discreet corner.

"All right, you're good," he said.

That's when Orion Pax emerged from the dolly, a smile spread across his face.

"Thanks, D. That was a close one...," Orion said, giving his best friend, D-16, a pat on the shoulder.

Chapter 2

D-16 pushed Orion into the wall of the train. "You listen to me, Orion Pax," he said.

"I'm listening," Orion said as he struggled to move against his friend's weight.

"This is the last time I save you," he said as he released his hold on Orion. "If you want to break protocol, that's fine. Go sneak into restricted areas, mess around in the archives, have at it. But I'm not covering for you anymore. I work too hard to risk losing it all because of your antics."

"C'mon, you know I'd never let you take the fall for me," he told his friend.

D-16 shook his head, unsure what to do about Orion.

"I know what I'm doing, D," Orion reassured.

"You're on your own," D-16 said.

Because Orion had such a strong interest in Cybertronian history, he couldn't understand how anyone could be so completely disinterested. He thought, *Maybe D is just pretending he doesn't want to know about Cybertron?*

"That's fine, I guess I won't tell you about the *Megatronus Prime* thing I found in the archives," Orion said, baiting D-16. As D-16's best friend, he knew that D-16's favorite Prime was Megatronus. D-16 turned back to face Orion, interested.

"What Megatronus thing?" he asked.

Orion attempted to hide his prideful smirk as he pulled out a Megatronus Prime decal, an illustration of Megatronus Prime's face.

"Just this mint condition Megatronus Prime decal, first edition. No big deal," Orion boasted. "I thought maybe you'd want it. Or I could just throw it away. I mean, Megatronus is your favorite Prime, right?"

Orion continued to bait his friend, and D-16 was having a really hard time not taking it.

"You know he's my favorite," D-16 murmured.

"Right, because he was the fastest?" Orion continued.

"No, because he was biggest and strongest! And you know that, too!" D-16 had completely taken Orion's bait. He was no longer mad at Orion; he just wanted the Megatronus decal.

"It's really cool. Thank you," D-16 said, sharing the same smile that sat on Orion's face.

"You're my best friend, D, and I've always got your back," Orion said, putting out a fist.

"No matter what," D-16 replied, completing the fist bump.

The train rumbled through Iacon City, taking D-16, Orion, and the other miners to a new Energon mine to begin working. For the rest of the ride, D-16 admired the Megatronus Prime decal his best friend had just gotten him, while Orion looked out the train's windows. He glimpsed a chain of residential complexes that were exclusive to Transformers robots, and once again, he felt unfortunate to be so young. Transformers bots not only had more abilities and options than any of the miners, but they also had more knowledge.

And they have memories that go back more than fifty cycles!

Orion sighed. Unlike Transformers robots, none of the miners could remember what their planet was like before the war with the Quintessons, before all Cybertronians were forced to move underground. Orion had heard Transformers bots talk about their memories of seeing skies overhead and seeing distant stars far beyond the skies. Even though Orion had also heard stories about how the war had completely destroyed the planet's surface and made it uninhabitable, he couldn't help regretting that he'd never seen stars, let alone the sky.

When Orion and the other miners arrived

at the mine, they were greeted by their crew leader, Elita-1. A cog-less bot, Elita-1 had shining neon pink armor, and she wore a jet pack.

After the miners put on their own jet packs and picked up additional mining tools and equipment, they flew after Elita-1 into a wide shaft. Elita-1 called up to control to request permission to begin drilling. Mining was hard and dangerous work, and Elita-1 always followed protocol.

The control room responded, "You're clear to dig, Elita-1. Good luck."

Elita-1 turned toward her crew and shouted, "Metal to the pedal, drill team! We got a fresh tunnel. The Energon should be soft and easy to break out."

As they moved into the tunnel, they installed extendable metal braces to support the surrounding walls and ceiling. Afterward, Elita and her crew landed in front of a blank metal wall. A moment later, a glowing vein of liquid Energon pulsed within the wall, causing the wall to shift and crack open. "Here we go!"

Elita exclaimed. "This one won't be open long, so brace it up!"

The crew moved more metal braces into position and slowly shifted the walls. As the braces groaned under the pressure, Elita told them, "Lower channel is open. Drill it out!"

Orion, D-16, and the others began drilling. But then a miner named Jazz got his drill bit jammed against the wall, and the recoil launched him backward to the floor. Everyone looked at the wall that he'd been drilling. Suddenly they noticed the Energon surge and fluctuate within the wall!

"It's unstable!" Orion yelled out. "We've got to move!"

"Evacuate!" Elita told them. "Everyone out! The tunnel is closing!"

The miners ignited their jet packs and were racing away from the unstable wall when a loud explosion tore through the tunnel. The explosion broke the abandoned braces and sprayed chunks of metal at the miners. The chunks struck Orion, D-16, and Jazz, and they crashed against the tunnel floor. Orion's jet pack slipped off his back and fell a short distance behind him. When Orion and D-16 pushed themselves up, they saw Jazz poking out from the rubble, pinned beneath a large metal boulder.

Orion activated his radio headset to communicate with Elita. "Jazz is stuck!" Orion yelled. "I'm falling back to assist."

"Negative!" Elita responded through her own headset as more explosions made the tunnel walls shudder. "Do not break protocol! Evacuate!"

Orion and D-16 pretended not to hear Elita. They raced back to Jazz, threw their bodies against the metal boulder, and shoved at it, trying to free their friend from the rubble. The boulder didn't budge.

"The tunnel's going to collapse!" Jazz said to Orion. "Grab your jet pack and go!"

Orion thought fast. He reached for his fallen jet pack. "Yeah, good idea," he said.

"What?" Jazz said. "No! I didn't mean it!"

"Gotcha!" Orion joked as he and D-16 grabbed hold of Jazz. Orion slammed the jet pack deep into the metal rubble. The combustible jet pack exploded on impact, blasting the rubble and boulder to bits. Orion and D-16 held tight to Jazz as the explosion launched them through the tunnel. They crashed and rolled against the tunnel's uneven floor while metal debris rained down on them.

Despite the loud noise, Orion heard Elita's voice on his headset. "Pax!" Elita called out. "Pax, what's happening?!" But before he could respond, Orion heard a faint whooshing sound grow quickly into a loud rumble. He realized the explosion must have opened a fissure in the cave. "Oh, that's not good," he shouted.

At that moment, a powerful gust of wind blasted through the tunnel and headed toward the three miners. Orion and D-16 saw that one of Jazz's legs was twisted, so they grabbed his arms and lifted him up. Jazz's injured leg dragged and bounced across the floor as his friends ran and hauled him forward.

Soon the tunnel was collapsing all around them. With Orion and D-16 supporting Jazz, they jumped over and ducked under a series of fractured braces. Looking ahead, they saw Elita just outside the tunnel's entrance. She picked up a brace and hurled it into the cave. The brace extended and caught a long section of the tunnel's ceiling, but the brace immediately buckled under the ceiling's weight.

Holding tight to Jazz, Orion and D-16 ran past the damaged brace. "Hurry!" Orion shouted.

"Not going to make it!" D-16 replied.

"Go, go, go, GO!" Orion demanded.

Elita jammed a fresh brace into the cave's unstable opening just as Orion, D-16, and Jazz stumbled out and collapsed beside her. An instant later, the brace snapped, and the metal walls slammed shut.

Orion and D-16 helped Jazz rise to his feet.

"Thanks, guys," Jazz said. "I thought I was a goner!"

Elita glared at Orion. "What's wrong with you, Pax?" she asked. "I told you to evacuate! If I get fired because of you . . ."

"Oh, please," Orion told her. "They're not going to fire you."

At that moment, a broad shadow swept over the group. Everyone looked up to see Darkwing, a full-size flying Transformers robot, descending toward them. Darkwing landed near Elita. "Elita-1, you're fired," he told her.

"What?!" Elita cried. *"Why?!* I followed the rules to the letter!"

"That is true," Orion agreed as he moved between Darkwing and Elita. He looked up at Darkwing. "*I* was the one who broke protocol."

Elita pushed Orion aside. "No one asked you, Pax!" she exclaimed. "Darkwing, *please.* I've worked too hard for this, you can't just—"

"You're all no-cog bots with limited

options," Darkwing interrupted. "Report to waste management. Immediately."

Elita-1's eyes widened. "Waste management?!" She gulped.

Orion could tell Elita was disappointed. "Elita . . . ," he began.

"Thanks for nothing," Elita whispered as she brushed past Orion and walked off.

"I'm sorry," Orion whispered back.

Darkwing turned to leave, a look of disdain on his face. "Hey, Darkwing," Orion said.

"Don't do it." D-16 already knew what his friends next move was going to be.

Orion ignored his friend's warning and continued. "Anyone ever tell you that you're as ugly as you are stupid?"

He threw a fist Orion's way. Orion ducked, D-16 caught the fist, and then both miners were trading loud, clanging blows with Darkwing.

The other miners wanted to avoid trouble with their Transformers supervisors, so they moved in quickly to break up the fight.

Chapter 3

While Jazz went to get his leg repaired, Orion and D-16 returned to their barracks. D-16 decided he needed to relieve some tension, so he began hitting a metal punching bag. Orion positioned himself on the other side of the bag and spotted D-16. "That was stupid, *really* stupid!" D-16 started. "I'm not coming to your rescue anymore," D-16 said as he continued pummeling the metal bag. "I could've been demoted!"

"Darkwing deserved it. Aren't you tired of being looked down on like we're nothing?"

D-16 let out a loud huff and pointed at his

ranking badge. "I can reach tier 11 by the end of this cycle. No miner's ever accomplished that. If you ruin this for me like you did Elita—" He punched the metal bag so hard that it made a loud reverberating noise. With the noise still echoing off the walls in the barracks, D-16 opened his fist and inspected his fingers.

Orion said, "What's the matter? You need a new hand?"

"I hope not," D-16 said. "I *like* this hand."

Suddenly a loud buzzer made all the miners in the barracks stop what they were doing. From the loudspeakers, a voice blared. "Attention, all sectors, active and off duty. Stand by for a live transmission from Sentinel Prime."

D-16 said, "Sentinel is back in Iacon already? Seems like yesterday that he left for the surface."

"Maybe he found the Matrix of Leadership!" Orion exclaimed. Remembering the data he'd discovered in the archives, he thought, *If Sentinel found the Matrix, Energon will flow freely on Cybertron, and we won't have to mine for it anymore!*

The miners turned their attention to the monitors that lined the walls of the barracks. On the monitors, images of Sentinel Prime, the leader of Iacon City, appeared. At the same moment, in the central area of the barracks, a large hologram of Sentinel flickered to life.

"Hello, my friends," Sentinel said, flexing his golden metal wings. "Hello, Iacon City. Hello to our saviors, the industrious miners who toil selflessly to maintain our Energon reserves. I celebrate you!"

The miners were ecstatic to hear such praise from Sentinel. Across the barracks, and also the mines and train platforms throughout Iacon City, all the miners cheered.

"Once again," Sentinel continued, "I have narrowly returned with my fleet after another treacherous expedition across the desolate, dangerous surface of our planet. I departed with hopes of finding the Matrix of Leadership, lost since our great war with the Quintessons. I regret to inform you that we've returned empty-handed."

Hearing that the Matrix of Leadership remained lost, Orion felt disappointed. *The Matrix has to be somewhere on Cybertron,* he thought. *It must be!*

"This is a setback," Sentinel told them, "but not a failure. Rest assured, I will find the Matrix of Leadership so that Energon can flow again. But that's in the future. Right now, I think we all deserve a little fun! Tomorrow, there will be no work. All shifts off, because tomorrow is . . . the Iacon 5000!"

Everyone knew the Iacon 5000 was an annual race, and the most anticipated sporting event on Cybertron. The race was only open to Transformers, but when the miners saw holographic symbols for the Iacon 5000 appear in the air, they roared with excitement.

Sentinel smiled. "My favorite event, a high-octane race all across Iacon City. Let's all see which competitor is *truly* more than meets the eye."

Just then Orion had an idea. A *brilliant* idea. As Sentinel's broadcast ended and the other miners turned away from the monitors and hologram projectors, Orion wondered how it was possible that no one had ever *had* the same idea. His idea was so fantastic that he couldn't stop thinking about it.

And hours later, after all the other bots in the barracks had gone to sleep, Orion decided that he absolutely had to wake up D-16 and share his idea. Immediately.

D-16 yawned as he followed Orion up a ladder and onto the roof of the barracks. "Whatever this is," D-16 said sleepily, "it better be good."

"Yeah, yeah, yeah, I know," Orion said. He led D-16 to an area of the roof that offered sweeping views of the city. "Okay, listen . . . What if, what if . . ." Orion directed D-16's gaze to an enormous, illuminated sign that promoted the Iacon 5000. "What *IF* . . . tomorrow *we* ran in the Iacon 5000?"

D-16 glanced at the sign and yawned again. "What if I sock you for waking me up?"

"No, no, no," Orion cried, "hear me out! We don't even have to win—"

"Oh, *that's* good," D-16 replied, "because we *wouldn't*."

"*But*," Orion said, "if we beat *just one* Transformer, it would change everything! Not only would we go down in history as the mining bots who achieved the impossible, but we . . . we would show *everyone* that we're capable of *so much more*!"

"Or," D-16 said, "we'd get publicly humiliated and then busted back to tier 1."

"Yeah," Orion admitted, "but at least we would've done *something*, you know?"

D-16 looked at Orion. He could tell from his expression that Orion was completely serious. But to D-16, the idea of entering the race was so ridiculous, he shook his head in disbelief.

"Pax," D-16 said.

Orion patted him on the back and said, "Come on, D, what—"

"Pax! We're mining bots who can't transform. We can't fly, we can't roll . . . we can't race," D-16 told him. "It's as simple as that. And now, I'm going back to sleep mode." He started moving across the roof, headed toward the ladder that extended down to the barracks.

"All right, fine," Orion said as D-16 sauntered off. "Yeah, maybe you're right."

But after D-16 was out of sight, Orion added, "Maybe."

Because Orion wasn't ready to give up on his idea.

Chapter 4

The next day, thousands of bots, all eager to attend the Iacon 5000, headed to an enormous stadium. However, two cog-less miners appeared to be walking in the wrong direction.

"Where are you going?" D-16 asked Orion. "The stadium's *that* way."

"Yeah, yeah, I know," Orion said. "Follow me."

As Orion led D-16 through a maintenance door in a restricted area of the stadium, D-16 said, "Great, we're going be late now. I wanted good seats."

The two friends descended into the dank,

dark underbelly of the city, which housed massive machines and automated maintenance systems. They moved past generators, rotating turbines, metal tubes, and slatted air vents, and were nearing a series of wide exhaust pipes when D-16 said, "I really don't want to miss the opening ceremony."

"Trust me, I know what I'm doing," Orion replied. But then he heard a loud, rushing rumble that was growing louder, like an approaching tornado. "Hold up!" he shouted.

Orion and D-16 ducked away from the wide pipes as a huge blast of exhaust whooshed out. The power of the blast surprised them and almost knocked them off their feet. "Wow," Orion said. "Get caught in one of those pipes, it'll launch you halfway across the city!"

D-16 sighed. "Where are you taking me?" he asked impatiently.

"Don't be a glitch," Orion said. "This will be totally worth it, trust me."

D-16 huffed as he followed Orion onto a suspended catwalk. But when they came to a stop, D-16 looked down and realized that the catwalk extended directly above the starting line for the Iacon 5000!

"You did this for me?" D-16 asked his friend, lost in complete wonder over their view.

"I did this for *us*," Orion replied.

At that moment, they heard a voice booming from the stadium's loudspeakers. "Let's have a big Iacon City welcome for today's competitors!" the announcer cheered.

From the catwalk, Orion and D-16 looked down to see dozens of Transformers step out onto the racetrack. The Transformers included the blue-armored Chromia and also the loathsome Darkwing.

The announcer bot said, "The moment you've all been waiting for . . . your host, Sentinel Prime!"

Sentinel Prime, his golden wings extended, swooped down from above the crowd before he came to a hovering stop in midair. "My friends, my Cybertronian family," he said. "It has been precisely fifty cycles since the Quintessons attacked our home. Fifty cycles since we lost the Matrix of Leadership, and our Energon supply dried up. Fifty cycles since the battle that wiped out the other Primes, my brothers and sisters in arms."

Around and above the stadium, thirteen massive holograms appeared. Each hologram represented a Prime who had not survived the Quintesson attack. When Orion saw the holograms appear, he thought again of the recording he'd seen in the archives. He glanced at D-16 and saw D-16's own gaze was locked on the hologram of Megatronus Prime, the biggest and toughest of the Primes.

"Today," Sentinel continued, "we honor the Primes who gave their lives for ours, and we show them that the strength of Cybertron will never be diminished." The holograms of the

Primes vanished. Sentinel landed on his personal platform in the stadium, and he gestured to the Transformers near the starting line. "Racers, on your marks!"

The racers shifted their body parts and changed to their alt modes. Although they ranged in size and color combinations, all were high-powered land vehicles and aircraft. On the catwalk above the racers, D-16 smiled as he looked down. He said, "I can't believe that we get to watch from the starting line, the best seats in the house!" Then he noticed Orion had moved closer beside him, and that Orion was carrying two jet packs. "Why'd you bring jet packs?" D-16 asked in bewilderment.

Sentinel said, "Get set!"

Orion strapped on a jet pack and said, "It's time to show them that we are more than meets the eye." Before D-16 could protest, Orion moved fast and slapped the second jet pack onto D-16's back.

Sentinel extended one of his arms, and it

changed into a cannon. The cannon fired with a thunderous *BOOM!*

"Oh no," D-16 muttered.

The catwalk automatically swung out from under Orion and D-16. They fell and landed on the starting line just as all the racers fired their own engines and jets and peeled out. Orion saw one racer speeding straight toward D-16. Orion grabbed D-16 and activated their jet packs, and then they were off, weaving around and between Transformers and into the breakneck competition.

The raceway was an automated track, a stretch of road that could instantly shift, twist, and change course. D-16 looked ahead and saw the track switch from a straightaway to a series of tight curves. D-16 risked a glance at Orion and said, "Are you crazy?!"

"Sure feels like it!" Orion exclaimed as he and D-16 soared over the curving track alongside their larger and more powerful competitors.

The announcer bot said, "The Iacon 5000 has begun!"

Sentinel, standing on his platform, leaned forward for a better view of the track and said, "Are those . . . *miners* in the race?"

Sentinel wasn't the only one in the stadium who'd noticed the two cog-less bots. "I can't believe what I'm seeing here! There are miners trying to run in the Iacon 5000! This is wild!" the announcer cried.

In the stadium's stands, astonished spectators turned their attention to the two bots, who appeared to be doing their best to keep up with the Transformers.

Elsewhere in Iacon City, Cybertronians were able to view the race on live broadcasts. Miners in the barracks, watching the race on holographic monitors, were stunned when they recognized the racing miners as Orion and D-16.

In a waste management distribution center, Elita-1 was loading crates when she looked at a nearby monitor and saw Orion and D-16 on the screen. She was so surprised that she almost dropped a crate on her foot. "You've got to be kidding me," she commented.

Orion and D-16 were still flying over the track, but they were far behind the other racers. The track suddenly changed course, twisting like a speeding snake through Iacon City. Orion and D-16 ignored the blurred lights of the surrounding towers and illuminated signs and kept their eyes on the track. Ahead of them, two Transformers failed to navigate a tight turn and spun out. Orion and D-16 swerved fast to avoid a collision.

Back at the stadium, a towering leaderboard displayed the names and standings of the racers. Spectators noticed the addition of the word "MINERS" at the bottom of the board.

The announcer said, "This is a first in Iacon 5000 history. How are they going to survive?"

On the track, something suddenly exploded

in front of D-16. "Hey, look out!" he yelled before he pulled Orion out of the way from the blast.

"I owe you one," Orion yelled out.

"More like a thousand!" D-16 replied. "I can't believe we're not in last place!" he yelled as he jumped off the road, following the course.

They raced on, passed through a checkpoint, and were still following the course when Darkwing swooped in, converting as he jumped through the sky, and struck D-16, knocking him off balance.

"Oooh!" the announcer bellowed. "A devastating blow!"

Orion veered over to D-16, tapped his elbow, and said, "Gotcha!" D-16 wobbled, regained his orientation, and flew on.

Another Transformers vehicle flew off the track. All the while, Orion and D-16 were climbing higher on the leaderboard. But as they soared into a tunnel lined with weapons that fired obstacles, they saw several jet-powered Transformers zoom past overhead.

More flying Transformers approached from behind. D-16 said, "We're not fast enough!"

"Improvise!" Orion shouted.

Orion angled up from the track and seized the edge of one Transformers bot's jet wing. The Transformers bot yelled, "Hey! Get off!" and kicked free of Orion's grip. D-16 caught Orion, but then another Transformers robot hit D-16 from behind, knocking D-16 and his jet pack off the track! More racers zoomed past Orion as he swooped over to help his friend get up.

The announcer said, "With the miners falling *waaaay* behind, we can now focus on the *real* contenders in this race. . . ."

But as Orion and D-16 looked at the Transformers who were heading away in the distance, they spotted a cluster of wide exhaust pipes. They recognized the pipes as the same type they'd noticed during their journey through the stadium's maintenance area.

Orion and D-16 looked at each other. They both had the same idea.

They quickly positioned themselves inside the exhaust pipes. A moment later, a great blast of air launched them out of the pipes and high across the city. They shouted as they soared past towering structures. Then they saw the track stretched out below them and angled their bodies downward.

Incredibly, they descended straight into a checkpoint. As they hurtled forward, they realized they passed through the checkpoint before most of the other racers, but then they saw Darkwing directly ahead of them. Unable to slow down, they accidentally clipped Darkwing, bending his rotors and causing him to veer off the track and crash.

"I don't believe it!" the announcer shouted. "The miners, from out of nowhere!"

Darkwing was still dizzy as he inspected his damaged parts, but there was nothing wrong with his vision or his memory. He knew who'd clipped him. He roared, "Miners!"

At the stadium on the leaderboard, "MINERS"

blinked up to the fifth position. The announcer said, "The miners are into the top five!"

All the cog-less bots in the stadium were on their feet, jumping and shouting and cheering for the two miners. Many Transformers among the spectators were also cheering. Few could recall a previous Iacon 5000 that was so exciting.

But the race wasn't over.

Orion and D-16 followed the four leading Transformers robots onto the last leg of the competition, a hazardous obstacle course. One of the leaders lost control, and the three other Transformers bots slammed into him. Broken Transformers parts went flying in all directions. Orion and D-16 swerved around the crashed Transformers and kept going.

"It's a four-bot pileup," the announcer said. "And . . . the two miners are now in first position. This is unbelievable!"

As "MINERS" blinked to the top position on the leaderboard, the crowd erupted in even louder cheers. Orion and D-16 sprinted forward onto the final stretch, a long, flat straightaway to the finish line. Neither noticed one stray piece of Transformers armor that was still soaring away from the pileup behind them until the piece smashed into D-16.

D-16 went sprawling and tumbled to a stop. Orion skidded and turned back to see one of D-16's legs bent at an odd angle and spraying sparks. When Orion moved to lift his fallen friend, D-16 said, "No! Go! Leave me!"

"No!" Orion shouted. "We do this *together*!" He slung D-16 onto his back and started running for the finish line. As he ran, his mechanical joints and gears strained at the impact of each step. He tried not to think about how exhausted he was, and how much D-16 weighed.

The announcer said, "One miner is now carrying the other, mere steps from the finish line! The most amazing, sensational, dramatic, heartrending, exciting, thrilling finish in the history of—"

Orion and D-16 were inches away from the finish line when suddenly Chromia hurtled past them. The force of her movement knocked Orion and D-16 aside, causing them to collapse upon the track. Lying flat on their backs, they craned their necks to see Chromia rapidly change to her bot mode before she slid across the finish line.

Chromia faced the spectators and pumped her fists in the air. The announcer said, "We have a winner! Chromia comes from behind to take the prize! Talk about an Iacon 5000 for the ages!"

Orion and D-16 were still lying on the track. "Well, *second place* is still pretty good," Orion said dryly.

But before they could even try crawling to the finish, all the remaining racers zoomed past the two miners. Orion realized the race was truly over for him and D-16. He sighed sadly.

D-16 frowned. He and Orion were mere miners, and they had entered the Iacon 5000 without any official approval. D-16 had no idea what would happen next, but he was certain that it wouldn't be *good*.

Chapter 5

"So," Orion said casually, "how long do you think we'll be here?"

"I'm not talking to you," D-16 snapped.

They were sitting on metal slabs in the Iacon 5000 stadium's medical facility. At other nearby slabs, Cybertronian medics and mechanics were busily repairing Transformers robots who had suffered damage during the race. One of the damaged competitors was Darkwing. D-16 glanced at Darkwing and couldn't help noticing that Darkwing was scowling at him.

D-16 looked at Orion and said, "I can't believe you made me do that. We're in so much trouble."

Orion shifted on his slab. "I thought you weren't talking to me."

"Hey, look," D-16 said, "I know it's all a big joke to you, but not me! I was paying my dues, I was going places . . . and now they're going to bust me down I don't know how many tiers!"

"I'm sorry, D," Orion said. "But . . . come on, didn't you feel it? Even for just a second, didn't you feel liberated? Didn't you feel like you were something else? Like you could be more than just what they say you are?"

D-16 looked at the floor. "Yeah, I felt it," he said. "I did." Then he lifted his gaze to face Orion. "But I *don't* remember agreeing to trade my whole life away for one second! Now we're forever going to be remembered as the idiots who embarrassed themselves in front of—"

The noise of clinking footsteps approaching made D-16 and Orion look to a wide doorway. They saw a tall black-metal Transformers bot enter the medical facility. They immediately recognized her as Sentinel Prime's surveillance officer. She had two arms, two legs, and four additional appendages that ended with sharp, tapered tips. She also had numerous optical sensors that allowed her to see everything around her without turning her head. Her name was Airachnid.

Airachnid looked at D-16 and Orion, and her eyelids clicked as she inspected the area. "It's clear," she said, then stepped aside, making space for the arrival of a much larger Transformers robot.

The sight of Sentinel Prime walking toward them left Orion and D-16 speechless. They slid off their slabs and stood at attention. Sentinel came to a stop in front of them.

"Orion Pax," Sentinel said. "D-16. What you two did today was one of the craziest things I've ever seen."

"Sir," Orion began, "this was all *my* idea, and we're so sorry we—"

"I *loved* it!" Sentinel exclaimed.

Surprised, Orion said, "You *did*?"

"How could anyone *not* love it?" Sentinel said. "You gave my best racers a real run for their money!"

D-16 said, "So we're not getting demoted?"

"Demoted?!" Sentinel chuckled. "The fact of the matter is, we're halfway into the first shift since the race ended, and that mining crew has already reached one hundred fifty percent peak quota. You inspired them to work harder!"

This is the opportunity I've been waiting for! Orion thought. "Sentinel Prime, sir, we joined the race to show everyone our potential. That we bots can do *more* than just mine Ener—" he began.

"Outstanding!" Sentinel interrupted. "I love a bot who can think for himself. Perhaps you two could tour the mines, speak to your brethren, and help them see their potential."

"Wow!" Orion said. "Great! That sounds incredible! I would love to be a—"

Ignoring Orion, Airachnid leaned close to Sentinel and said, "Sir. It's time."

"Ah yes," Sentinel said. He smiled as he looked down at Orion and D-16. "I'm sorry, friends. We're preparing our next travel to the surface. But in the meantime, I've got a treat for you! Hang tight." Sentinel nodded to Airachnid and said, "Have someone escort these heroes to my personal service facilities. Best care in Iacon."

Orion and D-16 could hardly believe what they'd just heard. Overwhelmed with happiness, they smiled at Sentinel. Sentinel grinned, aimed a long finger at them, and said, "Until next time, legends." He headed out the medical facility's exit, followed by Airachnid and her sharp, clinking feet.

D-16 shook his head in disbelief. "Sentinel Prime," he said slowly. "*The* Sentinel Prime!"

Orion said, "You still mad at me?"

D-16 thought for a moment. "I am *less* mad at you," he told him.

Orion chuckled. "I'm telling you, D, I've got a feeling that everything's going to change, and we're going to go—"

Before Orion could share his dreams for the future, a dark shadow fell across the area where he and D-16 stood. They turned to see Darkwing looming over them.

"Hi, Darkwing," Orion said.

Although medics had repaired Darkwing's damaged body parts, he did not look happy. Not one bit.

Chapter 6

"Wait, wait!" D-16 pleaded as Darkwing tossed him and Orion out of an elevator compartment and into a deep, dark chamber. "You don't understand! We were supposed to go to Sentinel Prime's personal service facilities!"

From the elevator, Darkwing said, "You two dolts are *never* going to see Sentinel Prime again. I'll make sure of that." The elevator door began to close.

"No!" D-16 cried out. "No!"

But the elevator door slammed shut, and Darkwing was gone.

"Ugh," Orion said. "I hate that guy."

Orion and D-16 were still adjusting their eyes to the darkness when they heard a noise from behind them. They whipped around and saw the silhouette of a bot standing near a fire that appeared to be burning within an oven or furnace.

The bot walked toward them. He was a small, cog-less bot. His face was concealed by a welding mask, and his yellow armor plating was covered with scorch marks and oily grime. Unlike Orion and D-16, the yellow bot did not have an identification badge.

Peering at Orion and D-16 through his mask, the yellow bot said, "How did you get down here? There's no access to this level! There is nobody down here but me!" Before Orion or D-16 could respond, the yellow bot said, "Oh my gosh, you're . . . *real*!" He raised his mask's visor to reveal his smiling face. "You're . . . you're . . . you're *others*, you're not me! You're *here*, and you're not me!"

"Uh, yeah," Orion said.

"Awesome!" the bot exclaimed. "I am so sorry—that must have been weird for you. I just . . . haven't had a lot of company since they put me down here in sublevel 50."

"50?" D-16 asked. "But there are only forty sublevels."

"That's what I thought! Turns out there are ten more, and they are *not* pleasant, probably why nobody ever really talks about them," the bot said.

Orion looked around at the chamber's rough, blackened metal walls. "How long have you been here?"

"How long have I been here?" the bot retorted. "Let's see, uh . . . somewhere between a long time and forever? I mean, I had other jobs, but I kept getting reassigned, because I'm so good at what I do. Oh! I'm B-127, by the way, but you can call me B."

"Great, great," D-16 said dismissively. "How do we get out of here?"

"Great question," B-127 said. "You don't."

D-16 said, "We don't?!"

"Nope!" B-127 said. "We have limited access to the waste management area, but the new shift manager there does *not* like distractions. No, no, they prefer we stay here, on the task at hand."

Confused, Orion said, "Uh . . . what is the task at hand?"

B-127 pointed overhead to a large garbage chute, just as a bunch of scrap metal and trash fell out of it. The scrap metal crashed down upon a conveyer belt, and the conveyer slowly carried the piles of refuse across the room to an open furnace. "Our job," B-127 said, "is to look for anything that might be worth salvaging before it hits the furnace and gets smelted."

D-16 said, "So . . . you watch garbage burn?"

"Yes!" B-127 replied with delight. "It is so great that you're here now! I can't wait to learn everything about you, and then tell you everything about me! I have a lot of hopes and dreams that I'm just dying to share with one or two new best friends."

"Uh, wow...cool...great," Orion replied slowly.

"Oh!" B-127 exclaimed. "Where are my manners? Come on, I'll introduce you to the rest of the crew." He led Orion and D-16 to a group of what appeared to be three odd-looking statues that stood beside a metal worktable. The statues were made of assorted bits of scrap metal, with body parts held together by bent wire and metal tape. "Hey, guys, we've got company!" B-127 announced. He gestured to each statue, one at a time. "This is EP-508, this is A-A-Tron, and this fella here is Steve."

"*Steve?*" Orion asked in confusion.

"Yeah," B-127 said in a hushed tone. "He's foreign."

"Uh, question... Do they talk back to you?" D-16 asked.

B-127 faced the statue that he called Steve. He said, "Um... they're not real. You think I'm *that* crazy?"

"Well," Orion said, "it's just that you've been down here—"

"I was *talking* to *Steve*," B-127 said. He patted the statue named Steve on the shoulder, and a bright light suddenly ignited in the statue's chest. And then, from the light source inside the statue, a strange, muffled voice said, *"Quintesson ambush!"*

B-127 chuckled as if Steve had just told a joke. "Ha! Classic Steve."

Orion leaned close to the statue, studying the bright light. "What is that?" he asked. "It's coming from inside." He touched the side of the statue and accidentally knocked the statue's head from its neck. The head fell, hit the metal worktable, and broke apart.

"Oh!" B-127 cried. "Steve! No! M'Steve!"

"I'm so sorry," Orion said as he examined the old bits of technology in the shattered head. He found a fragment of a compact beacon, a messenger device with a built-in holographic recorder projector. The device appeared to be mostly intact. "We can fix it," Orion said. He pressed a button. "Here . . ."

The device's lens projected a hologram of a bot with a garbled voice message. *"Quintesson ambush... Calling the High Guard for immediate support... for immediate support..."*

From his research in the Iacon City archives, Orion recognized the voice as well as the hologram of the bot, who had a distinctive array of magenta prongs that extended above his head. "That's Alpha Trion," Orion confirmed.

"One of the *Primes*?" D-16 asked.

"Repeat," Alpha Trion's hologram said. "Zeta Prime has fallen.... Must... protect... the Matrix... or Cybertron will *die*!"

Orion, D-16, and B-127 looked at one another with stunned expressions. B-127 muttered, "Holy Primus."

The recording continued. "Sending location coordinates. Sending location coord—"

A holographic map with numbered coordinates appeared above the projector. Orion analyzed the map and said, "Those are coordinates to a location on Cybertron's surface."

He pointed to a position on the map, a location on a high mountain. "This could be the place where the Primes perished in the Quintesson war. Which means this is where we could find . . . the Matrix of Leadership!"

"You trust this data?" D-16 asked. "It's . . . it's just a recording from an old beacon inside a statue made of garbage!"

"Or it's a clue," Orion told him, "of how we could find the Matrix!"

"Nope," D-16 said. "No way."

"Come on, D," Orion pleaded. He attached the messenger device to his own forearm. "This is our chance to show everyone—"

"Absolutely not!" D-16 interrupted. "You *already tried* to show everyone in the race you tricked me into running, which got us stuck down here in this *waste hole* with *this* . . ." D-16 looked at the small yellow bot, who was listening attentively. Not wanting to hurt B-127's feelings, D-16 said, "With this . . . uh . . . this really, really cool guy."

B-127 couldn't remember anyone ever calling him a cool guy. "Oh, thank you!" he said.

Orion turned to face D-16. "So I'm clear," Orion began, "which part are you mad about? When we inspired all the miners, or when we impressed Sentinel Prime?"

Before D-16 could respond, B-127 said, "You know Sentinel Prime?! You two have *really* seen some *stuff*!"

"Listen, D," Orion continued, "imagine if we helped Sentinel find the Matrix of Leadership. It would end the Energon shortage! No more mining. We could do whatever we want!"

"Yeah," D-16 said sarcastically, "*or* we go up to the surface and perish while searching for a magical lost relic. There's a *reason* no one goes to the surface. It's *dangerous*."

Orion shrugged. "Yeah," he said. "Yeah, you're right. We should stay here forever. That cool with you, B?"

"Forever?" B-127 asked. "This is great! I have new coworkers *and* roommates! There's plenty of room now that Steve has fallen apart. I usually sleep on the conveyer belt, but you can totally have it. I'll sleep in the corner next to A-A-Tron," B-127 said as he gently patted another statue friend he had made from parts of trash. "There's plenty of room for you guys to stretch out, too, because you're taller than I am. You know what I mean?"

D-16 let out a long groan. Orion sighed. He knew that D-16 had changed his mind, that he would rather risk a journey to Cybertron's surface than remain in an underground waste disposal chamber with the excessively chatty B-127.

"D, you won't regret this." Orion said. He picked up the old beacon and turned to B-127. "B, you can't live down here. Come with us. We could use your help finding a way to the surface."

"You kidding me?" B-127 asked. "The *surface*? Easy. I know a way!"

Chapter 7

"This is not as easy as I thought it would be," B-127 admitted. He was with Orion and D-16, inside the garbage chute, climbing up the chute's filthy, dented walls. When they finally reached the upper area of sublevel 50, B-127 said, "Only forty-nine more sublevels to go!"

"I regret this already," D-16 grumbled.

They climbed out of the chute and into an underground cavern that housed a depot for supply trains. All three bots remained in the shadows and out of sight. They looked down from their position and saw cog-less bots busily loading metallic cargo crates onto the cars at the backs of the trains, which sat on levitating tracks. Like the racetrack for the Iacon 5000, the train tracks could automatically extend, curve, climb, and descend between and around obstacles. Markings on the metallic crates indicated that the crates were filled with toxic waste.

"Waste disposal trains are the only vehicles that go all the way to the surface," B-127 told his friends.

"Yeah," D-16 said, "but they don't allow passengers. The trains are autonomous."

B-127 winced. "That's the 'won't be easy' part."

Orion studied one of the trains closely. "It's perfect. We'll be safe inside the train." He spotted a closed hatch atop one of the train's cars, and he motioned D-16 and B-127 to follow him to the hatch. They skulked across the car's roof, Orion opened the hatch, and they climbed down into the car. Inside the car, they ducked behind a stack of crates and hid from the cargo-loader bots. After the cargo-loaders finished their work and left the train, another bot entered to load one last cargo crate.

The bot was Elita-1. After securing the final cargo crate, Elita inspected the other crates, making sure they were properly secured and locked in place. Before leaving the train, Elita looked up and noticed an open hatch. Because she had inspected the train earlier, she knew that the hatch should have been closed. She moved below the hatch to examine it more closely and realized someone must have snuck onto the train.

She scanned the train car's interior for signs of an intruder. "Thanks for being so obvious, whoever you are," she said. "Turning you in will *definitely* get me promoted back up a rank or two—"

Still hiding with B-127 behind the crates, Orion and D-16 looked at each other anxiously. Both had recognized Elita's voice. Orion didn't want to cause any more trouble for Elita, but he was determined to go to Cybertron's surface and search for the Matrix. He signaled to D-16 and B-127 that they had to prevent Elita from capturing them.

D-16 wasted no time. He leaped out from behind a crate, tackled Elita, and shouted, "Got her!"

Elita kicked off a wall, and D-16 lost his grip. Elita flipped D-16 over, swept her leg out, and knocked him into the side of a crate. Orion and B-127 jumped out from their hiding place and tried to tackle Elita, but she quickly moved out of the way, and they both crashed to the floor.

B-127 cried, "Wait, wait, wait—"

"Elita, stop!" Orion demanded.

"Orion?!" Elita replied, clearly shocked.

"Hold on," Orion said as he tried to stand up. "Let me explain—"

Elita had no intention of listening to Orion. As the train started to rumble forward and leave the depot, she struck him and shouted into her headset, "Security! Sound the alarm!"

Then she ran through a door and entered the next car.

"She's headed to the engine!" D-16 yelled.

"Don't worry," Orion said. "I've got this!" He ran into the next car with D-16 and B-127 right behind him. They spotted Elita leaping over cargo crates and making her way forward. As the train gained speed, Orion shouted, "Hold on, Elita! Let me explain! We're on a mission!"

Elita shouted back, "So am I . . . to ruin your life!"

The front of the train suddenly tilted up at a sharp angle, and then the train and all its cars were traveling vertically, like a launched rocket, racing straight up through a long tunnel. Orion, D-16, and B-127 were unprepared for the abrupt change of direction. They tumbled, and grabbed at the secured crates to stop from falling. Elita jumped up and landed on the side of a cargo crate.

The train hurtled toward the top of the cavern that overlooked Iacon City. Elita unlocked the latches that secured the cargo crate beneath her and then leaped away. The crate went crashing into the path of her pursuers. "Look out!" D-16 shouted.

Orion dodged the crate and yelled, "Elita, wait! We found a message! We know where the Matrix—"

But Elita didn't listen. She opened a hatch and escaped to the roof of the train, which was still traveling straight up alongside the cavern's steep metal walls. Orion, D-16, and B-127 scrambled after her in pursuit, and the hatch slid shut behind them. There was no way back into the train.

They saw Elita climbing up the speeding train's exterior, making her way to the engine, and they climbed after her. B-127 glimpsed the cavern's walls whip past the speeding train, and he cried, "Why?! Why am I doing this?!"

"Climb faster!" D-16 shouted.

The four bots were still clinging to the train's roof when they zoomed up into a chasm and then entered a cloud of fog. None of them even noticed the increasingly heavy fog and change in atmosphere, when a sudden shift in gravity carried them horizontally out of the tunnel. The fog whizzed past them as Orion hauled himself forward across the train's roof. He extended one hand and managed to grab Elita's heel. "Gotcha!" he cheered.

Elita raised her fist and was about to strike Orion when the fog suddenly cleared. And then, for the first time in their lives, Elita, Orion, D-16, and B-127 saw the open sky and the surface of their own planet.

Cybertron's terrain featured many outcroppings and growths in strange geometric shapes, all highlighted by various colors and alloys. The train continued over the metal landscape while the four cog-less bots slowly stood up. In stunned silence, they gazed at their surroundings.

They saw jagged sheets of glittering metal that appeared to slowly shift and rise from the surface to form frozen, angular waves. Distant shimmering lights danced on the horizon, and Orion looked up to see millions of small lights across the sky. For his entire life, he'd been told that Cybertron's surface was treacherous and uninhabitable. He never imagined the surface would be so magnificent.

"The surface . . . ?" D-16 said in awe.

"It's beautiful," Elita said.

The train continued over the planet's surface, and the stars appeared to wink out as a large sun began to rise. B-127 looked around and watched the sunlight illuminate rolling metal hills and valleys and cast long shadows of metal mountains across sparkling metal sands. He was overwhelmed by the view. "I am . . . speechless," B-127 marveled.

Orion noticed Elita was no longer poised to hit him. "Elita," he said, "listen to me. We know where the Matrix of Leadership is."

"Oh, sure," Elita said, "and *I'm* really a Prime. I just prefer loading crates of toxic waste . . ."

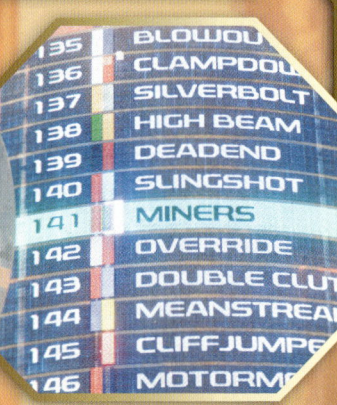

135	BLOWOUT
136	CLAMPDOWN
137	SILVERBOLT
138	HIGH BEAM
139	DEADEND
140	SLINGSHOT
141	MINERS
142	OVERRIDE
143	DOUBLE CLUTCH
144	MEANSTREAK
145	CLIFFJUMPER
146	MOTORMASTER

Orion held out the compact beacon that he'd attached to his forearm. He activated the beacon so Elita could see Alpha Trion's holographic message and the map with the coordinates.

Elita's eyes widened. "Whoa," she said. "Where did you get this?"

"From my friend Steve," B-127 said. "Orion knocked his head off."

Orion sighed. "I didn't knock Steve's head off on purpose."

D-16 leaned close to Elita and said, "Steve was not alive."

"What?" Elita said.

"Never mind," Orion said. "Sentinel told us he was going to the surface, and *then* we found this message. We figured we could hand-deliver it to him or scout the location ourselves, whichever comes first." Orion held the beacon out for Elita's inspection. "This was too important to wait. It will change all our lives."

Elita looked at the beacon for a few seconds before she shook her head. "No, no, no," she said. "I'm not going to get demoted *again* because of you, Orion. I'm turning this rig around and notifying the proper authorities about—"

"Uh, guys," D-16 interrupted. "What is that?"

The others followed D-16's gaze. They saw an enormous wave of metal dust that appeared to be growing taller and wider on the horizon. They quickly realized the wave was approaching from across the glittering plains. They could also clearly see that the wave was heading straight for the train!

"Get back inside the train!" Orion demanded. "Hurry!" They turned and ran back across the train's roof until they arrived at the nearest hatch. B-127 and Orion bent down and tried to open it, but the emergency control latch wouldn't budge.

D-16 and Elita moved beside the others to help, but as they pressed and pulled at the hatch, D-16 turned his head and saw the metal wave rising fast in front of the train. He said, "Oh, *now* I know why no one comes to the surface!"

The metal wave struck, lifting the train and its cars high above the plains. The train's automated tracks extended to form a descending curve, which sent the train down past jagged outcroppings. The four bots were still hanging on to the train's roof when a deluge of metal sand crested and crashed, tossing the four bots off the roof. As the train shuddered against the wave's impact, it sent the train car and the bots tumbling until they plunged into dark, sloping dunes of metal sand and debris.

The train continued on without them.

Chapter 8

After Orion and D-16 managed to dig themselves out from the metal sand, they heard B-127's muffled voice calling for help. They found him buried headfirst in a nearby dune. While D-16 grabbed B-127's legs and pulled him free, Orion spotted Elita's body lying on another dune. Elita wasn't moving, and her eyes were closed. Orion ran to her side, crouched down, and said, "Elita? Elita!"

Elita's eyes opened.

"You okay?" Orion asked.

Elita was disoriented, but she threw a strike that landed on Orion. She pushed herself up from the sand, struggled to her feet, and looked around. "The train!" she cried. "Where's the train?!"

Orion looked toward a distant, rising trail of dust. Elita followed his gaze and saw the train zooming away across the metal wastes. She had been hoping the train would carry her back to Iacon City. She let out a harrowing scream.

As Elita's scream echoed across the barren landscape, Orion held out his forearm-mounted beacon and projected the holographic map. He pointed to a section of it and said, "Okay, so I *think* this is where we are, and if we follow this path to that mountain—"

Elita snatched the beacon from Orion and glared at him. "Okay," she said, "now *you* listen to *me*, Mr. Zero Seconds Since My Last Accident! I'll go on your little quest because I don't have a choice. But *I* carry the map, *I* navigate, and if this leads to nothing, then *I'm* dragging you and those two tin-headed go-bots back to Iacon City and to the first supervisor depot we see, at which point you will explain everything that's happened using words that reflect me in a very positive light! Got it?"

Orion nodded. "Yeah," he said. "Okay, deal, great, all right."

"Let's go!" Elita said. She started walking.

B-127 brushed metal sand from his arms as he fell into step beside Elita. "Hi there," B-127 said. "Uh, *Elita*, yes? Am I saying your name right? I, uh, wanted to formally introduce myself. I'm B-127, but you . . . you can call me B if you want, or—"

"I'm going to need you to talk less," Elita said.

"Oh, sure, no, yeah, no problem," B-127 stammered as he fell in line behind her.

"Hey, guys," Orion said, "check it out." He pointed to a hill that was covered with something green, something that resembled fine, soft blades that extended up from the ground.

A light breeze in the air caused the green blades to sway back and forth. Orion stepped over to the bottom of another hill and said, "There's more of it over here."

Elita and D-16 bent down to examine the blades.

"What is it?" Elita wondered.

"It's not metal," D-16 told them.

"So weird," Orion said. "It looks like it's growing, like some kind of, uh . . . nature?"

They looked up from the field of green blades and saw a herd of unusual robo-deer creatures moving over the hill. Each one had four legs and sharp, pointed antlers. The creatures lowered their heads to the soft blades on the ground and opened and closed their mouths.

"Whatever that green stuff is, those things are eating it," Elita said.

B-127 cringed. "Ew! That's gross!"

Just then, a loud *BOOM* sounded from across the plains. The four-legged creatures raised their heads, and a bright red hue flowed suddenly through their antlers. The herd took off, scattering away from the field.

"What was that noise?" Elita asked. Before anyone could answer, a sudden gust of wind swept over the hills and whipped at the four bots!

"Something's not right," Orion said as he watched the antlered creatures run toward a cluster of old, ruined structures. "We should go."

"Yeah," D-16 agreed. "Good idea."

Elita looked up and spotted a dark object traveling across the hazy sky. The object was a spaceship with strange, spiky weapons. "Run!" Elita shouted. She sprinted after the fleeing herd.

As Orion and the other bots followed her, he noticed the ruins had distinctive Cybertronian architectural details and metalwork. Large rusted pipes and girders, fragments of long conveyers, and collapsed hangars and garages indicated the structures had once been part of an industrial complex. Orion wondered if the original structures had been destroyed during some long-ago battle between the Transformers and the Quintessons.

The bots entered the ruins and quickly tried to conceal themselves amid the large pipes and abandoned machinery. They peeked out from their hiding places, looked up, and saw the spaceship hovering overhead. B-127 pointed to the ship and said, "Is that . . . ?"

"A Quintesson scout ship," Elita whispered.

Orion signaled everyone to be quiet and not move. But then the Quintesson ship projected hundreds of red beams of light down across the area, then they moved and drifted over the nearby hills. The crisscrossing beams shifted and spread out over the ruins. As they scanned over the hull of a building, one of the antlered creatures darted out from behind a rusted metal sheet that was leaning against the building's outer wall. The creature tried to avoid the sweeping beams, but it was not successful.

BOOM!

The creature was gone, obliterated by the ship's lasers.

Orion saw more red beams drifting toward the area where he and his allies had concealed themselves. "The ship is scanning for life-forms. Move!" he warned the group.

The four bots ran through the derelict complex, weaving around and jumping over metal debris to avoid the deadly lasers. B-127 slipped and stumbled, but Orion grabbed his arm and helped him up. They saw D-16 and Elita ahead of them, running for cover in a long nook under a metal outcropping.

Orion was still tugging B-127 alongside him when he glanced back to see a tangle of red beams closing in fast from behind. He knew that he and B-127 couldn't run fast enough to reach the nook that protected D-16 and Elita. He saw a narrow metal support beam that spanned two tall girders, and he ran for it, pulling B-127 into the shadows beneath the buttress.

But B-127 couldn't stop fast enough, and his momentum nearly carried him straight through the open area between the girders and under the threat of the red beams. Orion dug his own feet into the ground and tried not to lose his balance as he gripped B-127, whose weight threatened to cause both of them to fall forward.

The lasers were all around them, moving across the top of the buttress and the sides of the girders. B-127 wobbled and Orion lost his grip. B-127 started to fall, but Orion reached out fast, caught B-127's arm, and held tight.

The Quintesson ship's beams turned off. A moment after the ship began moving across the sky and away from the area, Orion and B-127 collapsed on the ground. Orion thought, *That was way too close!*

Watching the ship leave, B-127 asked, "What were they searching for?"

D-16 rolled his eyes. "Someone to *hug*, B. How should I know?!"

"Let's not wait around to find out," Orion commented.

Elita consulted the holographic map before she lifted her gaze to an imposing metal mountain with dark peaks. "This way," she said. "We're close." She started running toward the mountain, and the others followed.

Sharp metallic rocks and more green blades littered the mountain's foothills. The bots proceeded carefully. As they crested a ledge, D-16 felt a strange chill and said, "Anyone else getting the feeling that something is really wrong up here?"

They stumbled upon the jagged mouth of a cave. Long, tapered sheets of sharp metal jutted out from every angle of the cave's walls, floor, and ceiling.

"A cave with teeth," B-127 quipped. "Nothing scary about that." He tried to sound brave but tried harder not to tremble.

Elita checked the holographic map again, then tossed the beacon to Orion, who reattached the device to his forearm. As Elita led the group into the cave, B-127 looked up and said, "Knives coming out of the ceiling. Amazing. Everyone, do we have to go inside?" No one answered. Against his better judgment, B-127 decided to follow them. "Okay, yep," he said, "we're going in. Why shouldn't we? Just walking into the scariest place I've ever seen in my life."

The four bots activated their mining headlamps. D-16 led the group deeper into the metal-walled cave and into a series of dark chambers. In one chamber, Orion saw an ancient rifle lying on the floor. He looked up to see that the walls were riddled with laser scorches.

The passages became more and more narrow. They soon discovered that the only way they could continue was to shove rubble aside as they crawled on their hands and knees.

Eventually they emerged on the floor of a large cave. Shafts of natural light extended through holes in the cave's ceiling and illuminated the dark chamber. They stood up and looked around.

The cave contained the shattered, rusted remains of the thirteen Primes. Orion, D-16, Elita, and B-127 had struggled for many hours to reach their destination, but they were not prepared for the immense sadness that they felt upon finding the Primes' ruined metal bodies.

They moved slowly into the tomb. The Primes' remains were buried under heavy layers of the natural flora and fauna of Cybertron. As D-16 approached the remains of his hero, Megatronus Prime, he thought of how often he'd wished he could have met him. D-16 lowered his head in respect.

Orion walked over to all that was left of his own hero, Zeta Prime. After he looked at Zeta's broken head and torso, he noticed the empty socket at the center of Zeta's chest.

"The Matrix of Leadership," Orion realized. "It's gone!"

Chapter 9

Orion, D-16, Elita, and B-127 began searching the tomb for any sign of the missing Matrix of Leadership. Orion gazed among the remains, and from the corner of his eye he noticed a dim, blinking light under fallen metal rubble. He called his allies over, and they all began to pull the rubble away, uncovering a large Prime who had suffered heavy damage. However, the Prime's body was mostly intact, and the light in his chest continued to blink.

B-127 realized the Prime was the same one from the recording that Orion had recovered from Steve. "It's Alpha Trion," he said.

Orion examined the blinking light. "He's powered down," he said, "but his spark . . . it's still lit."

As every Cybertronian knew, a spark was what gave life to bots, but bots also required Energon to stay alive, and most carried emergency supplies. B-127 removed an Energon tube from a compartment in his left arm and handed it to Orion who inserted the glowing blue cube into Alpha Trion's mouth.

Immediately a faint blue glow appeared within Alpha Trion's neck. The glow slowly spread as the Energon charged up some of the ancient Prime's circuits. Sparks shot out from Alpha Trion's sides and joints, causing Orion and B-127 to jump back.

"Go, go!" Alpha Trion's voice crackled. His head and body jerked, and his eyes went wide. "Under attack! Attack! Iacon City! Message before—"

"Whoa, whoa," Orion said, as he moved closer to the Prime. "It's okay, it's okay! You're safe now. The war's over." He hoped to calm Alpha Trion.

Alpha Trion studied the four bots who were staring at him, and he then realized he wasn't in danger. He pushed his damaged body up from the ground, and his rusted mechanical servers made grinding noises as he limped across the tomb and knelt beside the remains of Zeta Prime.

"I failed you, old friend," Alpha Trion said sadly. "You deserved so much better than this end." He turned his gaze upward toward the other fallen Primes that scattered the cave.

From behind Alpha Trion, Orion said, "No. You didn't fail."

Alpha Trion turned to look again at the four bots. Orion attempted to explain. "We heard your message. We've come to find the Matri—"

"Your conversion cogs," Alpha Trion said alarmingly. "What *happened* to you?" He was gazing at the hollow sockets in each bot's chest. "Who *are* you?"

"We're cog-less miners," D-16 said, "from Iacon."

"Miners? Why?" Alpha Trion asked, his curiosity and confusion growing.

"We've had to drill for Energon ever since it stopped flowing," Elita answered.

Alpha Trion's head rattled as he shook it. "Impossible!"

"That's why we came," Orion said, "to fix things. If we find the Matrix of Leadership, and get it to Sentinel Prime—"

"*Sentinel,*" Alpha Trion interrupted, "is *no Prime.*"

Now the four bots were confused. "What are you talking about? Why would you say that?" Orion asked.

"Sentinel Prime defeated the Quintessons. He saved all of us!" D-16 continued.

"No," Alpha Trion said, "you have not been saved. You've been living a lie. I saw the truth with my own eyes. Come. I will show you."

The four bots watched as Alpha Trion

reached down to touch the colorful metallic dust on the floor of the cave. Under the powerful Prime's control, the dust lifted and swirled around in the air, and then the dust took shapes that were formed from Alpha Trion's memories. The bots watched with amazement as dust became ghostly images of the thirteen Primes meeting with Sentinel on a war-torn battlefield.

"For thousands of cycles," Alpha Trion began, "the war with the Quintessons had been a brutal conflict. Until Sentinel, the principal aid to the Primes, intercepted an enemy transmission. There was going to be a secret gathering of Quintesson commanders. Their elimination could end the war. It was a mission so important, we Primes took it on ourselves. We agreed to meet Sentinel for his sensitive intel in secret, here in this cave. But we were not alone."

The metallic recollection from Alpha Trion's memory of the Primes showed the Primes looking up. The four bots looked up too. Overhead, the colorful dust had formed into a swarm of skittering claws and countless Quintessons descending with their weapons aimed at the Primes. The Primes began fighting back.

"We were outnumbered," Alpha Trion continued, "but we stood as one. Our victory was near . . . until we were betrayed."

The four bots watched in shock as Alpha Trion's memory showed Sentinel sending his Primax blade through the back of a Prime. They saw Megatronus Prime try to protect Zeta Prime from a horde of Quintessons, but then Sentinel used his Primax blade once again to cut down Megatronus. Seeing the treacherous Sentinel's actions, D-16 felt a great rage rise up within him.

Alpha Trion's memory continued and showed Sentinel picking up a fallen rifle. Sentinel fired at the remaining Primes and helped the Quintessons destroy the greatest heroes of Cybertron. After Zeta Prime fell to his knees, Zeta looked up at the traitor and gasped, "Sentinel, . . . why?"

Sentinel sneered. "For all the power on Cybertron," he said. He drew his cosmic rust gun and fired. There was a bright flash, and then Zeta Prime, the leader of Cybertron, fell to the ground.

But the Matrix of Leadership glowed bright in Zeta Prime's chest. Sentinel reached down, tore out the Matrix, and held it triumphantly.

Alpha Trion said, "But Sentinel never understood the true power of what he desired. The Matrix of Leadership can only be wielded by one who Primus himself deems worthy . . . and Sentinel, most certainly, was not."

The four bots watched the image of the Matrix glow brighter, and then it radiated so much energy that Sentinel could no longer hold it. "NO!" Sentinel yelled. At that moment, the Matrix appeared to explode, sending metal dust in all directions.

The images disappeared, and the metal dust fell and settled on the floor of the cave. Orion looked at Alpha Trion and said, "Hold on. You're saying the Matrix of Leadership . . . just vanished?"

Before Alpha Trion could reply, D-16 said, "No . . . no, *that* is impossible! I don't believe it."

"Why would Sentinel do that?" Elita asked.

"To make a bargain," the Prime told her, "with the *new* rulers of Cybertron."

Suddenly, an incredibly loud rumbling noise came from outside, and debris started falling from the cave's ceiling. The four bots rushed to the fragile Alpha Trion and helped him to the cave's entrance. Then they made their way to the ridge right outside of the cave. From the ridge, they looked down to a valley to see several Cybertronian supply trains come to a halt near one another. Among the trains was the one that had delivered the four bots to the planet's surface.

The rumbling grew louder, and dozens of

Quintesson scout ships emerged across the sky. As the scout ships circled the area, an enormous vessel, a Quintesson mother ship bristling with weapons, began to descend to the planet's surface. The mother ship resembled a monstrous, bulbous beast, and it expelled a foul stench as it moved through Cybertron's atmosphere.

The mother ship had just touched down near the trains when a group of flying Transformers robots arrived from across the valley. The Transformers bots changed to their bot modes before they flipped and landed in front of the ship. The leader of the group was Sentinel Prime. He was accompanied by the multi-eyed Airachnid and several squadrons of Trackers, winged Transformers bots who served as Sentinel's enforcers.

The mother ship's cargo bay door dropped open, and a moment later, the Quintesson High Commander and their escort of multilegged Quintesson guards poured out. The High

Commander had a large, wedgelike head that dominated most of their upper body, under which dangled long, writhing metal tentacles.

The High Commander hovered to a stop in front of Sentinel. Sentinel bowed his head and kneeled before the High Commander. Airachnid and the other Transformers robots did the same.

Watching from the ridge, Orion, D-16, Elita, and B-127 were outraged and horrified by the sight of Sentinel yielding to the Quintessons. Then they saw Sentinel gesture to the supply trains, and the trains began to automatically unload their cargo.

Elita recognized the crates and said, "I loaded those crates. They're filled with contaminated metal."

"I don't understand," Orion said. "What do the Quintessons want with toxic waste?"

The Quintesson mother ship began to hum before it projected an energy field at the crates. The crates lifted into the air, and then their outer casings ruptured and fell away, revealing that each crate contained a gleaming Energon cube.

"Our Energon!" D-16 said with fury. He started to rise from his hiding place on the ridge.

Orion pulled his friend back. "Stay still, D."

The cog-less bots returned their attention to the figures outside the mother ship just as the Quintesson High Commander grabbed Sentinel and lifted him off his feet. Sentinel strained against the High Commander's clutches and said, "I know what I promised you, but our mines . . . they're running out. There's barely enough Energon for us."

The High Commander let out a loud, menacing hiss before they eased their grip and let Sentinel fall to the ground. Sentinel said, "I swear, I will get you the rest."

The Quintesson guards escorted the High Commander back into the mother ship. As the mother ship and the scout ships lifted away,

Sentinel glared at Airachnid and his other Transformers soldiers and said, "Double-time every mining shift! I want more Energon, now! Let's go!"

After Sentinel and his soldiers flew off, Alpha Trion and the cog-less bots returned to the center of the cave that had become the final resting place for the other Primes. "Now you have seen the truth," Alpha Trion said.

"I knew it," Orion said in frustration. "Deep down, I always felt something was off! Cybertron is dying, and all this time, Sentinel has us mining Energon that he gives to our sworn enemy."

Elita was fuming. "Sentinel bought himself power, and then put us to work paying off his debt."

"I can't believe it," B-127 said. "Well, obviously, I *can* believe it because I just saw it, but . . . I still can't believe it."

Orion shook his head. "It was all a sham. How could we have been so gullible? Oh, this . . . *this* is going to change everything!"

D-16 whirled on Orion and snapped, "You just *had* to do it, didn't you?!"

"*Me?*" Orion said. "What did *I* do?"

"You just had to go to the surface," D-16 said angrily, "had to enter the Iacon 5000. You just had to break protocol!"

"Who cares about protocol?" Orion said.

"I do!" D-16 shouted. "*I* care! Because nothing bad happens when you stay on protocol!"

"Sentinel Prime has been forcing us to work in the mines until our gears strip, and all the while, he's been giving the Energon away to our greatest enemies," Orion replied, trying to steady his voice.

D-16 laughed. "Uh, and what do you think he's going to do to us when he finds out that we know his secret?"

"I'm not thinking about what *he's* going to do," Orion said. "I'm thinking about what *we're* going to do."

"Fantastic," D-16 replied with contempt,

"*another* Orion Pax master plan. I can't wait to hear this."

Orion was confused by D-16's reaction. "Don't you want to stop Sentinel?" he asked.

"No." D-16's eyes suddenly flashed bright red. "I want to crush him! I want to put Sentinel in chains and march him through the mines so everyone can see him for the *false* Prime that he is. I want him to suffer. But we all know that it doesn't matter what I want, right, Pax? The fact is . . . we're just cog-less bots. Right?" D-16 chuckled. "We had limited options, and now . . . now we have *none*."

Alpha Trion limped forward to position himself between the arguing friends. "No child of Cybertron is born without a cog," he said.

"Oh yeah?" D-16 said. "I've been with myself since I came online, and *this* slot's *always* been empty!" He banged his fist against the hollow socket on his own broad chest.

Elita looked up at Alpha Trion and said,

"So, what are you saying? You're saying that Sentinel—"

"No, no way," B-127 interrupted. "Nobody could be *that* evil, not even Sentinel."

Alpha Trion confirmed their fears. "Sentinel removed your cogs *before* you came online," he said. "What better way to control a workforce with limited options."

Orion suddenly felt ill. "We were born with conversion cogs, but Sentinel—"

"He took them from us!" D-16 fumed.

Alpha Trion moved across the cave so that he stood closer to the remains of four fallen Primes. "What defines a Transformer," the Prime said, "is not the cog in their chest, but the *spark* that resides in their core. A spark that gives you the will to make your world better. My fellow Primes had that spark . . . and I see their strength in you. Take their cogs and access your full potential."

Alpha Trion closed his eyes and lowered his frail body to kneel on the cave's floor. The walls trembled, and the cave crackled with energy as Alpha Trion used his remaining strength to summon a mystical magnetic force. "Prima. Onyx. Alchemist. Micronus," Alpha Trion called out. "Warriors of noble spirit, loyalty, strength. Their uniqueness enhanced . . . by these." In the chests of the four nearby Primes, the cogs began to glow and then levitated out of their sockets. The cogs drifted through the air and moved toward Orion, D-16, Elita, and B-127.

Onyx Prime's cog inserted itself into D-16's chest. Prima's cog positioned itself perfectly in Orion's chest. Alchemist Prime's cog attached itself to Elita. And Micronus Prime's cog went to B-127.

The four cogs rotated, locked into place, and began radiating energy. Power surged through the bots' circuits, and their gears and armor made whirring and clanking noises as their frames grew and expanded. Within seconds, Orion, D-16, Elita, and B-127 had become full-size Transformers robots, each one stronger than they ever could have imagined.

Alpha Trion opened his eyes and gazed upon the four new Transformers bots. He gestured to the fallen Primes and said, "*They* were one." He held his hands out to Orion, D-16, Elita, and B-127 and said, "*You* are one.... *All* are one. Let their power flow through you and feel your true potential."

Before the four new Transformers could respond, the sound of distant explosions reached the cave. A moment later, the cave's walls shook, and metal dust and shards fell from the ceiling.

Alpha Trion knew the feeling all too well. They were under attack. "Sentinel's forces have found us!" he yelled.

Chapter 10

A ripple of louder explosions made Orion and his allies realize Sentinel's forces were blasting at the mountainside in a violent effort to break through to the cave. D-16 raised his new, larger metal hands, curled his fingers into fists, and said, "Time to fight back."

"No," Alpha Trion said. "You must return to Iacon City and alert the others." Alpha Trion raised his hands and again used his conjuring powers to pull metallic dust from the ground. The swirling dust transformed into images of Sentinel betraying the Primes. Alpha Trion flicked his fingers, and the images spun and twisted into the beacon on Orion's forearm. Alpha Trion gestured to the messenger device and said, "Embedded in this are the records I have shown you. Use it to reveal the truth."

"We will," Orion said with a bow.

Alpha Trion pointed to a dark hole in the cave's wall. "This tunnel," he said, "leads to the mountains. Cybertron's future is in your hands."

The group heard more explosions and rumbling from outside the cave. "We're out of time," Elita said. "We've got to move!" She started running for the tunnel with D-16 and B-127 right behind her.

But Orion didn't budge. "Wait," he said, looking at Alpha Trion. "We . . . we can't just leave you here."

Alpha Trion placed a hand on Orion's shoulder. "Your fight will come, my friend. Primus has a purpose for us all—" A thunderous *BOOM* interrupted Alpha Trion and rocked the cave. As more debris fell from the ceiling and walls,

Alpha Trion said, "But *this* fight . . . this fight is *mine*. Now, go!"

Orion nodded, turned, and ran fast, following Elita, D-16, and B-127 into the tunnel. When he caught up with them, he said, "We need to hurry!"

As they approached the tunnel's exit, D-16 turned to his friends and boasted, "I still think we have better odds fighting than outrunning them."

"Wait," Elita called out to her fellow bots. "We have cogs! We can Transform now!" she said as she pointed a thumb at her chest.

"That's right!" Orion said. "Everyone ready?"

"I was *born* ready," Elita said.

"On three," Orion said. "One—"

A massive explosion tore through the mountain, and the tunnel floor dropped out from beneath Orion and his allies. They fell and rolled down a hill, tumbling alongside metal boulders until they came to rest on the floor of a valley below. From their position, they could only hear Sentinel's Trackers firing their arm-mounted cannons at the mountain, but they knew the Trackers must be getting closer.

D-16 pushed himself up from the rubble, pointed to the cog in his chest, and said, "How do we use these things?!"

"I don't know!" Orion shouted back. "Just . . . *try*!" He started running down the valley, and the others followed. As he ran, Orion felt a few pieces of his armor plating start to shift and change shape. "It's working," he said. "It's working!" But when sections of Orion's head unfolded and threw him off balance, he yelled, "D! Help! Ahhhh!"

D-16 was experiencing troubles of his own, specifically that one of his feet had changed into a tank tread. As he kicked at the ground with his other foot, he wobbled and muttered, "This . . . is not . . . faster!"

Meanwhile, one of Elita's legs had changed into a spinning tire that began dragging her along the ground on her back. She let out a loud yelp when she accidentally collided with B-127.

Orion, D-16, Elita, and B-127 were still trying to figure out how to change into their vehicle modes when they heard weapons firing from behind, and then metal projectiles smashed into the ground all around them. They glanced back just in time to see Sentinel's Trackers in their bot modes, running down the valley. The Trackers jumped and swiftly changed into aircraft. They fired more projectiles as they rapidly descended over the valley.

B-127 moved one of his arms to shield himself from the Trackers' barrage. Much to his surprise, his body had somehow suddenly transformed into a yellow race car, but he realized he was missing some vital parts. "Wheels!" he said. "I need wheels!"

The four bots struggled to haul their partially transformed bodies toward a thicket of metal trees, where they hoped to take cover from the Trackers. But when Orion, D-16, Elita, and B-127 ran out from the grove and arrived in a clearing, several Trackers dropped down directly in front of them.

Orion was still running when he decided to leap at the Trackers. As he leaped, his body parts shifted, flipped, and folded, changing him into a Cybertronian semitruck.

At the same moment, Elita changed into a sleek motorcycle, and she swerved and popped a wheelie. D-16 grinned as he changed into a massive tank. And B-127's wheels dropped below him, and he drove straight for the Trackers.

Before the Trackers could move, the four approaching Transformers vehicles struck, crushed, and flattened their enemies.

Orion, Elita, and B-127 stopped and changed quickly back to their bot modes. "We survived!" Orion cheered.

Elita echoed her friend's enthusiasm. "That was incredible! I have wheels inside my legs!"

And to no one's surprise, B-127 couldn't

hide his excitement. "Did you see me slide all over? I have no idea what I'm doing, and I love it!" B-127 said with a smile.

The three bots failed to notice a Tracker who had avoided being crushed. The Tracker stood up and aimed one of his arm cannons at Orion.

KA-BOOOOM!

The noise made Orion, Elita, and B-127 jump. They turned to see the scorched remains of the Tracker, and then they noticed D-16 was still in his tank mode. His cannon was smoking.

D-16 changed to his bot mode, strolled over to the ruined Tracker, and then began stomping on the few remaining pieces of the Tracker's armor. D-16 said, "Didn't see *that* coming, *did* you?!"

Orion hurried over and tried to gently pull D-16 away from the wrecked Tracker. "Okay, okay," Orion said, trying to calm D-16. "I, um . . . I think you got him."

"Oh yeah, I got him!" D-16 said. He looked

back toward the mountains and bellowed, "I'll get 'em all; send whoever you got! Send 'em all—I will take on any bot and send 'em offline!"

Orion's eyes widened. He'd never seen D-16 so worked up. "Whoa, buddy," Orion said. "Are you okay?"

"I'm great!" D-16 said, and clapped one hand on Orion's shoulder. "*Cogs!* We did it! We have *cogs!*" He punched Orion in the chest plate. "We're wasting time. We have to get back to Iacon."

Orion reached to his forearm and activated the beacon to project the holographic map and said, "Looks like the fastest way back to Iacon is—"

"I got it," D-16 said as he snatched the messenger device from Orion.

Orion noticed a pinch of metal dust spill out of the device. "Be careful!" he said. "Our evidence against Sentinel is inside that—"

"I got it!" D-16 snarled.

Orion instinctively backed up. He glanced

at Elita and B-127. Both appeared surprised by D-16's behavior.

D-16 checked the map. "Iacon's this way," he said, his voice back to normal. "Follow me." He converted to his tank mode and began moving fast away from the others, heading toward the outer edge of a wide expanse of metal trees.

Elita and B-127 looked at Orion with caution, but then each changed to their vehicle modes. They followed D-16's trail of tread marks into a dark metal forest.

Chapter 11

Night was falling, and D-16 was still leading Orion, Elita, and B-127 through the dense jungle on Cybertron's surface. Because of the uneven metal ground and the narrow paths, they had to travel in their bot modes.

D-16 arrived at a cliff. He moved onto a metal ledge that descended to the jungle floor. As D-16 proceeded downward, Orion motioned for Elita and B-127 to stop beside him. Elita saw the concern in Orion's expression and said, "So, D-16 is . . . different."

"Oh really?" Orion said without humor. "You noticed?"

"I like the way he's different!" B-127 said. "He's dark and intense, and I'm glad he's on my side."

The group followed D-16 down the cliff and deeper into the jungle. When Orion noticed that D-16 was walking so fast that he was leaving everyone else behind, Orion walked faster to catch up with him. Orion said, "Hey, D, you want to stop for a minute?"

Without looking back, D-16 said, "Why would I want to stop?"

"I just wanted to see how you're doing," Orion said. "You were worried about what was *going* to happen, and then *a lot* happened, and now—"

"And now I feel amazing!" D-16 exclaimed. "Primus blessed us all with cogs. I can finally *do* something."

"Oh," Orion said. "And . . . what do you intend to do?"

"I will crush Sentinel Prime and any bot that ever stood with him."

Elita gasped. "You're not serious?" she asked.

"Sentinel's a traitor," D-16 said. "He ruined our lives."

Elita moved in front of D-16, gazed at him sternly, and said, "And bringing Sentinel down will reverse everything that's happened?"

"It's what he deserves!" D-16 said, fuming.

"D's right," Orion said. "Sentinel deserves everything that's coming to him."

"What?" D-16 said, surprised that Orion seemed to agree with him.

"Primus gave us cogs and the chance to expose Sentinel to all of Iacon," Orion started. "*That's* how we bring Sentinel down . . . with the *truth*," he finished.

Angry again, D-16 turned and snapped at Orion, "Who do you think you are?"

I think I'm your friend, Orion thought, but he doubted D-16 really cared to hear that at the moment. Instead he said, "D, we're in a position to make a real difference. I want to help build a better Cybertron, not just punish the bot who ruined it."

D-16 snickered. "Fine," he said. "That's fine. I'm strong enough to take down Sentinel myself. I don't need *this* . . ." He reached to his forearm and removed the beacon that he'd taken from Orion. "Because *this*," D-16 said, "won't save anyone."

Orion looked from the messenger device to D-16. He wondered if D-16 was about to destroy the device. Orion extended his hand and tried to sound calm as he said, "I think I should take that from here."

"Come get it," D-16 said coolly.

Orion looked at his friend worriedly and said, "Don't do this—"

"Come on, Pax," D-16 taunted. "Stand up for what you believe in. Take it from me."

Elita considered stepping between the two bots but decided that might be a dangerously bad idea. "Guys, can we take it down a notch?" she said.

Orion kept his eyes fixed on D-16 and said, "I'm not going to ask you again."

"Or what?" D-16 said with a menacing leer. "What are you waiting for? Take it."

Orion was gearing up to make his move when dozens of electric darts zipped out from behind the surrounding metal trees. The darts struck Orion, D-16, Elita, and B-127, and shocked them with powerful waves of electricity, knocking them out instantly. They never even had time to wonder who had fired the darts before they collapsed to the ground.

They were still unconscious when their large, mysterious attackers moved out from behind the metal trees, grabbed their ankles, and hauled them into the dark jungle.

Where are you? Airachnid thought.

She'd been searching for the four bots for hours, ever since she and Sentinel had taken care of the feeble Alpha Trion in his foul cave.

She and Sentinel had learned that the four bots had visited Alpha Trion but escaped the Trackers' assault on the cave.

When she'd left the cave and mountain, she'd found the remains of her ruined Trackers. She also found fresh tracks left by the new Transformers robot vehicles. The tracks convinced her that Alpha Trion had given conversion cogs to the bots. Orion Pax, D-16, and two other bots were now equipped with cogs, and they were on the run.

She followed their trail into the jungle. But after she descended a metal cliff that brought her to a lower area of the jungle, the tracks seemed to vanish. She closed her electronic eyes, bent backward, and opened the concealed compartments on her head to reveal hundreds of extra eyes and other sensors.

She scanned the ground and spotted something unusual.

Specks of metal dust, the same type that she'd seen on the floor of the cave that contained the fallen Primes. Scanning farther, she found tracks that she didn't recognize. She studied the tracks and determined that Orion Pax and his allies had been attacked and dragged away.

"Found you," Airachnid said out loud.

She looked up from the tracks, adjusted and extended her arms and legs, and leaped up to the jungle canopy. She grabbed at the high leaves and tore across the metal trees, heading after the four Transformers robots and their unidentified captors.

Chapter 12

Orion, D-16, Elita, and B-127 were still unconscious when a tall Transformers robot looked at another and said, "All right, wake them up."

A long shock stick jabbed at the sleeping Transformers, jolting them awake one by one. Their eyes opened, and they realized they were kneeling on the floor of a large, dark, smelly chamber. Orion noticed that the lower half of B-127's face was covered by a strip of metal. He realized the metal strip was a gag and that someone had welded it over B-127's mouth.

Orion looked around. Despite the darkness in the chamber, he was pretty sure they were inside a derelict Cybertronian ship, and he could see that his group was surrounded by dozens of tall Transformers robots. One had blue gauntlets, a red chest plate, and retracted wings at his back, and because he sat on a makeshift throne, Orion assumed he was the leader. Standing to one side of the leader was a purple-armored Transformer whose head housed a yellow electronic eye. On the leader's other side was a blue-and-silver bot with a shoulder-mounted cannon and a boxy chest that housed a bizarre array of sensors. All the Transformers robots in the chamber wielded heavy weapons.

The seated leader faced Orion and said, "Now, are you spies, or just incompetent lackeys?"

"We're not spies!" Orion said defensively.

Elita tilted her chin at Orion and said, "But he *is* incompetent,"

Then the Transformer with the boxy chest directed his sophisticated sensors at Orion.

"Scanning electrical impulses," the bot said. "He speaks the truth."

"Bah!" The seated leader slammed a fist down upon the side of his throne. "That just means he believes *himself*, like any spy would."

B-127 tried to speak, but his voice was muffled by the metal strip across his mouth. "Why is he gagged?" Elita asked.

"He wouldn't stop talking," said the purple Transformer with the yellow eye.

"Even when he was unconscious?" Elita asked, though not very surprised.

"*Especially* when he was unconscious!" the purple Transformer said.

"Enough!" said the leader. He leaned forward on his throne to make sure he had the full attention of the captured Transformers robots. "Two options for you. *One*, we slowly dismantle each of you, one bolt and screw at a time, and really make sure you feel it."

B-127 heard power tools being activated on the far side of the room, and he cringed. He reached to his face and started tugging at the metal gag.

"Or," the throned leader continued, "*two*, in exchange for a quick death, you give us intel on the Energon trains, access to the mines, or anything else that could hurt your boss, Sentinel Prime."

"Wait, what?!" Elita said. "Who exactly are you guys?"

Just then, B-127 managed to remove the metal gag, and he said, "The Cybertronian High Guard!"

The purple Transformer looked at his friend with the boxy chest and said, "I *told* you the gag wasn't tight enough!"

B-127 looked to his three friends as he gestured at the Transformers who surrounded them. "They're the High Guard," B-127 said, "prestigious defenders of Iacon!"

"*Prestigious?*" Elita said in disbelief.

"B is right," Orion said. He bowed his head to the Transformer on the throne and the others beside him. "You *are* the High Guard. I read all about you in the archives. You were truly exalted warriors."

Unable to contain his enthusiasm, B-127 pointed at the Transformer on the throne and said, "Look! That's Starscream." He then gestured to his friend with the boxy chest and the Transformer with the yellow eye. "And you're Shockwave . . . and Soundwave. Gosh, raise your hand if 'wave' is in your name! There's a lotta waves in here—"

"Silence!" Starscream bellowed. "The yellow annoying one is correct. We were once the High Guard. We witnessed Sentinel's betrayal, saw the Primes fall. Since that day, we've been fighting from the shadows, doing whatever we can to sabotage Sentinel."

"That's great!" Orion said as he started to stand up. "We're—" He froze when he heard, from all around the dark chamber, the sound of countless weapons locking, loading, and charging. He realized all the weapons were aimed at him, and he held up his hands.

"Whoa, whoa, whoa, whoa!" Orion said. "Okay, okay! We're good. Everyone relax." Keeping his hands elevated, he faced Starscream. "I'm just saying we're all allies! We were on our way back to Iacon, and now with your help, we can unify Cybertron against Sentinel Prime."

Starscream laughed, and then all the members of the High Guard were also laughing loudly. When they were done, Starscream shook his head and said, "The idea of a unified Cybertron is a myth. All that counts is the strength of one bot over another!"

The High Guard responded with loud cheers. B-127 leaned close to Elita and said, "Okay, so these guys are a little intense."

"Yeah," Elita said, "just a little."

D-16 had not said a single word since he'd awakened in the High Guard hideout. He rose to his feet, turned his back to Starscream, and started to walk away.

"Hey!" Starscream called out. "What're you doing?!"

A group of eight High Guard soldiers moved in front of D-16 and formed a wall of Transformers to stop him from leaving. They didn't intimidate D-16 one bit. "I'll tell you what I'm *not* doing," D-16 said as he turned to face Starscream. "I'm not cowering in some busted ship, playing king of the throne. I'm not pretending like I'm making a difference by throwing one punch and then running away to hide. Today I found out that Sentinel is rotten, and I'm going to make him pay for it . . . *today!*"

Starscream stepped down from his throne and strode over to D-16. He said, "You think you can insult me and just walk away? No one leaves here unless *I* say so."

"Is that right?" D-16 asked. "Well, how can you say so with my head in your face?"

WHAM! D-16 had leaned forward fast, sending his metal head hard against Starscream's forehead. All the Transformers in the chamber were so startled by the sight and sound of the impact that they instinctively jerked their own heads back.

But for D-16, the fight had just begun. Starscream shoved D-16 back. D-16 recovered and pounced, and then they were both striking each other and crashing across the floor of the chamber. The High Guard soldiers enjoyed seeing fights; they started shouting and cheering, egging on Starscream and D-16 to continue.

Not everyone in the chamber was so encouraging. "D!" Orion yelled. "Stop!"

D-16 didn't listen. His metal fists hammered at Starscream, then he lifted Starscream off his feet and swung him down against the floor. When the fight-loving High Guard soldiers saw their leader lying crumpled near D-16's feet, they began chanting. "D-16! D-16! D-16! D-16! D-16! D-16!"

D-16 pumped his fists above his head and let his gaze sweep over the surrounding soldiers. He said, "You want to see the strength of one bot over another? Huh?!"

From the floor, Starscream struggled to

raise his hands as he looked up at D-16. Starscream's voice sounded high and squeaky as he gasped, "Please . . . stop . . ."

D-16 was about to bring his fist down again on Starscream when his arm unexpectedly changed into a large cannon. Seeing the cannon, D-16 smiled with admiration. He lowered his arm and aimed his cannon at Starscream.

"Please," Starscream said in his high-pitched voice, "I beg you . . ."

Orion took a cautious step toward D-16 and said, "D, he's *not* the enemy!" Orion wasn't sure if D-16 was even listening to him, but a moment later, D-16 reluctantly pulled his cannon away.

D-16 again turned his attention to the crowd. "Bear witness!" he said. "This is the last time I show mercy! You want revenge? Decide right now." He gestured to Starscream, who remained sprawled on the floor. "Stay here in hiding, bowing before your pathetic leader, or follow *me* as we march on Iacon, and I take down Sentinel once and for all!"

The High Guard soldiers roared in approval and resumed chanting D-16's name. They began stomping their feet, and soon their entire hideout was quaking and shaking.

Orion noticed a red glint flash in D-16's eyes, and he became even more concerned for his old friend. He'd always known D-16 to have a competitive edge, but now it was more than competitiveness.

He's become so different, Orion thought. *So . . . violent.*

The hideout was quaking so hard that debris started falling from above. Orion looked up and saw cracks and holes in the ceiling, and through the gaps he saw sharp-winged bots swooping down from the night sky.

Trackers!

And then Airachnid's forces attacked.

Chapter 13

An explosion tore through the High Guard hideout's ceiling, blasting twisted fragments of hot metal in all directions. The blast knocked Transformers off their feet, and many accidentally dropped their weapons. A large rifle fell near Orion. He grabbed the rifle and threw it to D-16.

D-16 caught the weapon. Orion changed into his alt mode, a semitruck, and D-16 leaped up onto his back. D-16 saw Trackers pouring in through the roof's mangled frame, and he opened fire.

Airachnid and a group of Trackers landed

on the ground and began shooting at the High Guard. D-16 saw Trackers move in front of Orion, he jumped away from Orion and converted into his tank mode. D-16's cannon thundered as he blasted at the Trackers.

Orion changed back to his bot mode and ran after the nearest group of Trackers. D-16 decided the moment was right to change back to his own bot mode, but just as his tank parts flipped and retracted into his body, Airachnid sprang and tackled him. She held tight to his wriggling body as she hauled him up through the hideout's ruined ceiling and into the air.

Elita was fighting off three Trackers when Orion saw her change from her motorcycle mode to her bot mode. Behind Elita, a Tracker launched a missile and Orion yelled, "Elita, get down!"

Orion shoved Elita out of the way a split second before the missile could strike. But Orion hadn't cleared the missiles range. The missile exploded right next to Orion and sent him and large chunks of the hideout's floor flying, along with any Trackers in its way. Then everything went dark for Orion.

It took Elita most of the morning to dig Orion Pax out from under the ruins of the High Guard hideout. When she finally pulled Orion free, he lifted his gaze and said, "I feel like someone dropped a cliff on me. Where are the others?"

"Sentinel's troops took as many prisoners as they could carry," Elita said. "They got D-16 and B, and also half of those High Guard hotheads."

Propping himself up on one elbow, Orion looked around to see the remaining High Guard soldiers helping one another out of the rubble. Then he remembered the messenger device that Alpha Trion had given him. He looked to his forearm and saw the device was broken, and all the red dust had spilled out. He removed the device and chucked it aside. "Our proof against Sentinel," he said, "it's gone."

"So," Elita began, "what do we do now?"

Orion shook his head. "I think maybe D was right."

"Right about what?" Elita asked.

"Everything," Orion said. "Look around." He gestured at the surrounding ruins. "This is a disaster, and it's all my fault. I should have stayed on protocol."

Elita knelt down beside Orion and looked him in the eye. "Listen to me," she said. "I really want you to hear this. Are you listening?"

Orion nodded.

"I'm better than you," Elita said.

"Yeah, okay," Orion said with a smirk. "I'm hearing you."

"I'm better than you in every way," Elita continued, "except . . . you have *hope*. You always have. You went back into the mine to rescue Jazz. You snuck up to the surface to find the Matrix of Leadership."

Orion shook his head. "And how did *that* work out?" he snickered.

"My point is that your instincts tell you to break protocol for a reason. This blind optimism you have is why you make such bold and courageous choices, that are also extremely irrational. You're inspiring—you can envision a better future that no one else can see. And if we ever want to see B and D-16 again, *that's* the Orion Pax we need right now."

Orion allowed Elita's words to sink in, and then he began to think of a plan. "Those Energon trains will be heading back to Iacon. If we intercepted one—"

"I can reroute it." Elita said. "What else do we need?"

Orion rose from the ground and looked to the nearby area where Shockwave and Soundwave stood with the remaining High Guard soldiers. "Well," Orion said, "my bold instincts tell me we have to recruit some hotheads."

Elita sighed. "I was afraid you'd say that."

Elita walked alongside Orion as they made

their way over to Shockwave, Soundwave, and the others. "High Guard," Orion said, "in order to save our captured comrades, we have to act now."

"I have a better idea," Shockwave said. "How about I blast you back to Iacon?"

Shockwave never saw Elita's fist coming, but he felt it. "Ouch!" he cried. "She hit me!" Shockwave said in disbelief.

"Everyone be quiet," Elita said. "*All* of you. Listen to Orion."

The High Guard troops sullenly turned to face Orion. "Most likely," Orion began, "Sentinel will be keeping his prisoners at the top of Iacon Tower. A surprise attack will give us a chance to rescue them."

"Why should we follow *you*?" Shockwave said with contempt.

Elita took a step closer to Shockwave and clenched her fist. Shockwave noticed Elita's fist by her side, quickly gave his attention to Orion, and said, "We will follow you."

Soundwave nodded at Orion, "What is your plan?"

Orion looked in the direction that led to Iacon City. "We roll out."

The High Guard soldiers didn't budge. But then from the back of the group a soldier said, "What did he say?"

Elita leaned close to Orion and said, "Louder."

Orion saw that all the soldiers were now giving him their full attention. He also realized that he had, at least for the moment, become their leader.

And so he raised his voice to give his first order: *"Transform and roll out!"*

The battle for freedom had begun.